PROTECTING HIS WINDFLOWER

A Spirit Hunters Series Novel
Book One

Temperance Dawn

Copyright © 2020 Temperance Dawn

All rights reserved

This book is a work of fiction. References to real people, events, establishments, organizations, or locations are intended only to provide a sense of authenticity and are used fictitiously. The characters and events portrayed in this book are fictitious and are a figment of the author's imagination. Any similarity to real persons, living or dead, is coincidental and not intended by the author. Though several places and events mentioned within the story are historically correct, the story is fiction that the author has created for entertainment purposes only.

No part of this book may be reproduced, or stored in a retrieval system, or transmitted in any form or by any means, electronic, mechanical, photocopying, recording, or otherwise, without express written permission of the publisher.

ISBN: 9798689244426 (paperback)

Cover photo courtesy of: G-Stock Studio/Shutterstock.com
Cover design by: Maja Kopunovic
Written by: Temperance Dawn
Published by: Temperance Dawn
Edited and Proofread by: Nicolette Beebe

Printed in the United States of America

For Chike, because there's no such thing as a final draft.

Godspeed, my friend.

There is no reason not to follow your heart.

-Steve Jobs

PROTECTING HIS WINDFLOWER

A Spirit Hunters Series Novel
Book One

Temperance Dawn

One

Heavy footsteps charged up the grand stairs. Wood splintered as three men kicked the door in. Liam was pulled from bed, tossed to the ground as if he were nothing more than refuse. Whimpering sounds had him scampering to his feet only to be halted by a blow of solid knuckles cracking against his cheekbone. Blood oozed from his flesh. The scent of iron flooded his nose. Shock dulled the sting at first but quickly morphed into a piercing pain, sending stars shooting off behind his eyes. Two sets of hands lifted him from under the armpits and shuffled him out of the bedroom and down the hallway, his feet dragging behind him.

In the study, the men stepped away from him. Liam's eyes darted around the room, spotting two burly men through his cloudy vision. His beloved was near the door. Her hands were bound behind her, and a rag covered her mouth. Each of the two men held her by an arm. Unable to fully focus, another blow to his ribs rocked him to his core. He hunched over and clutched his middle before falling to the floor. Gasping for air, he was rocked by a fiery pain hitting his temple. More blood seeped from his head, pooling onto the wooden planks beneath him, staining the rich chestnut floors. The room spun as cries echoed in his ringing ears.

Liam rolled to his side. His vision blurred when he cracked his eyelids open. The dim light sent stabbing pains through his head. Weight pressed him into the floor while his hands were bound with rope behind him. His love being restrained across the room sent his heart into an agonized panic.

Only moments ago, he had been staring into her brilliant honey eyes. The golden flecks danced in the warm glow of the candlelight. His hands had been tangled in her wavy, mahogany hair. Now, tears streamed down her cheeks in constant waves. Her luscious, rosy lips trapped behind a cloth. He wanted nothing more than to go to her, crash his mouth onto hers, and swallow her pain away.

Another set of footsteps echoed from the hall. The sight of pointed toe, black boots came into view. The man donned an ornate walking stick and coat. His back faced Liam as he removed his top hat and spoke. "What is this I see?" his voice, deep and menacing. Liam had heard the voice many times. Only he didn't know who the man was, couldn't ever place his name.

The man touched his fiancé's hand, lifting it into his, and glared at the exquisite gold ring he had placed on her finger only moments before.

Liam coughed and willed his head to rise, to look into the eyes of the man holding his bride to be captive. "Don't touch her!" Liam rasped.

"Does this mean you said, yes?" the man asked her. His hand grasped her chin, forcing her to look at him.

Her confirming nod wobbled, but her eyes held a definite and firm stare.

"You know *I* could have given you more? All of this could

have been ours. We could have lived together."

A muffled shout ripped through her, followed by a scream of agony when the man's walking stick landed on the side of her head.

"No!" Liam bellowed.

"Take her away!" the man shouted before removing the engagement ring from her finger, placing it in his breast pocket.

Liam bolted to his feet as the two men dragged her out of the study and down the stairs. Her screams were muffled by the gag. But his movement was halted as a set of firm hands held his shoulders in place. The man with the familiar voice turned toward him. His eyes were dark and full of hatred. The sneer on his mouth was not that of a man, but that of something…evil.

Liam's heart raced, and his mind struggled to find a solution as the room went dark.

No sounds.

No light.

Only total darkness filled his senses.

Liam frantically opened his eyes and found himself in his bedroom, sweaty and panting from the nightmare he had to endure for the hundredth time. The late afternoon light cast shadows from the trees outside on his walls, where they danced to the rhythm of the wind. His body felt lifeless, as it always did after he woke from the dream. As if the life-force had been drained from him.

That recurring nightmare plagued him for all of his adult life. He suffered the tormenting dream time and time again. Lately, the dreams came more frequently, and he couldn't put his finger on the reason. However, there was more information in this episode. The woman he loved in the dream was his fiancé. A piece of knowledge that squeezed his heart. He hadn't been able to rescue her. The nightmare always ended the same way, in total darkness before he could reach her.

Sitting up on the edge of the bed, Liam stood and walked to the bathroom. Cupping his hands under the running faucet, he splashed his face in an attempt to wash the images from his mind. He watched the water cascade over his pale skin and stubbled jaw while staring at himself in the mirror. His eyes were red and swollen from tears.

Something was different this time. The pull felt stronger, keeping him in the undercurrent of the dream far longer than he had ever been in it before, making it difficult to wake. The woman felt more real. The pain in her eyes hit him with a force that could only be shared between two lovers, not a fantasy. "It's only a dream."

Two

Five o'clock PM. Right on schedule, Emily thought to herself as she stepped onto the pavement, glimpsing at the mass of low clouds in the distance. Clicking the key fob in her hand to lock her sky blue hatchback, she turned to the North as a breeze picked up. The view of the Golden Gate Bridge in the distance, standing tall and mighty, greeted her. A symbol, she had read, of perseverance and determination. It seemed fitting that she felt compelled to take up residence in the spectacular city.

The fog made its way into the Bay, creeping ever so slowly toward the entrance of the Golden Gate. It would glide through the narrow channel beneath the towering bridge and blanket the entire city in a thick, pillowy, grey mass. Growing up in Seattle, Emily was used to dark, damp skies and welcomed the coolness that freshened the air. Her only reservation about her new residence was the ominous presence she felt growing stronger.

Turning toward the historic Victorian home that she now lived in, Emily gasped before letting out a huff of air in annoyance. The front window to her flat swayed open in the gentle wind. A window that had continuously been opening even though she was adamant about ensuring it was closed and locked before leaving. Emily made a mental note to stop by the caretaker's unit that evening and ask if he could take a look at it.

A heaviness bared down on her as she climbed the steps to the front door of the old building. The house sat sandwiched between two other row houses in the center of the block. It was a typical architecture style used in San Francisco to build more large, single-family style homes during the nineteenth century.

The charming, two-story Victorian home had been converted into two separate residential units years ago. She lived on the main level of the building while the caretaker, who she hadn't yet met, lived in the top unit. Her front, living room window was flush with the house, but the unit above had a rounded, larger window with beautiful carving detail framing it. The traditional Victorian era, steep pointed roofline adorning the top, drew her eyes up to view the majesty of the home. It was evident that the house had once been painted in bright colors of royal blue, gold, and amethyst. But time and the salty air of the city had weathered its vibrance.

Dark oak wood paneling stopped a third of the way up the walls. High ceilings showcased the same chestnut crown molding woodwork. Faded tan paint created a stark contrast between the walls and ceiling. And, a heavy, rounded wooden framed staircase greeted Emily as she passed the threshold. Above the front door, the stained glass window cast a colorful warm glow in the morning while the sun shone through—a once elegant and formal entry now worn by time and lack of care.

The door to Emily's flat was on the right. The large staircase leading to the upper level sat halfway down the hall. A second set of stairs, through a wooden door, led to the basement.

She lifted her key and inserted it into the deadbolt when a man coming down the stairs caught her eye. He was tall, maybe six feet, with dark hair and a closely shaved beard framed his strong jaw. Dark rimmed glasses accentuated intensely blue eyes. Though his all-black attire added to his brooding mystery, he smiled and waved as he walked toward her.

He paused, hesitating for a split second when their eyes met as he finished the last few strides to her. His gaze warmed her insides, sending her heart into a gallop and flipping her stomach until her breath caught.

The man towered over her as he approached, coming to a stop only a couple of steps from her. "Hi. I'm Liam Wesley. You must be Emily Taylor."

The sound of his voice was hypnotizing. It was smooth and deep, sending the butterflies in her stomach into a frantic frenzy. "Yes. I am." Emily cleared her throat while tucking a lock of curls behind her ear. "I just moved in a couple weeks ago. Are you the caretaker that Phil mentioned?"

Emily's new landlord, Phil, had informed her that the tenant above her took care of all the maintenance in the building and she should contact him with any issues she may have. The convenience of an on-site caretaker only added to the attractiveness of the rental. As soon as Phil responded that the unit was available for immediate occupancy, Emily signed the lease agreement and began the moving process.

"That would be me. I travel a lot for work, and I just got back into town today. I'm sorry I wasn't here to welcome you for the last two weeks. My work has been quite busy. It's nice to finally meet you." He held out his hand, and Emily took it.

"Very nice to meet you," Emily echoed, saying a silent prayer that she wasn't turning beet red from the blush creeping up her face.

"I'm glad to see someone finally living here. It will be nice to have a neighbor again."

Curious at Liam's statement, Emily asked, "How long was the place empty?"

"About six months. Phil just can't seem to find reliable tenants. I know he was worried about dropping the rent price, afraid he'd only get shoddy people inquiring."

"Oh. I can assure you I'm not shoddy. I'm a quiet person, there won't be any loud parties or any commotion coming from my place. Plus, I don't know anyone here in the city yet, so I won't be having company anytime soon." Emily stared down at her keys, embarrassed that she'd already shared so much information with a perfect stranger. Albeit, her incredibly attractive new neighbor, but a stranger nonetheless. Willing the moment to pass quickly, she fumbled for her key, clutching it between her thumb and finger.

"Oh, no. Please don't take that the wrong way." Liam took a small step toward her. "Phil sounded very happy when he told me you would be moving in. Don't worry. You might hear a couple of my friends from time to time. We work together, so we occasionally meet up here to talk business, but we're not party animals. You said you don't know anyone around here. May I ask, where did you move from?"

Emily pulled in a breath. "Seattle," she admitted.

Liam's eyes lit up as he smiled down at her. They were the color of crystal clear waters with light and dark tones dancing together, creating a kaleidoscope effect as she gazed into them. "Seattle? Really? I've been up there a few times. Great city."

"Yes. It's a great place to live." Seattle had been the only home Emily had known until a couple of weeks ago. She was more than ready to restart her life in a new city and forget about all of the heartache from her past. Though the darkness still lingered near her, an element she wasn't sure she would ever be able to escape.

"Actually, I'm glad we ran into each other. I was just thinking of heading upstairs to introduce myself to you."

"Oh yeah? I came by to do the same a bit earlier, but you weren't home. Do you always keep your window open when you're gone?" Liam's ocean eyes brightened. His mouth tipped into a sexy grin.

"Umm...My front window seems to be swinging open a lot. I know I close it *and* latch it. I even triple checked before I left this morning," Emily giggled at the absurdity of it. She was nervous. She knew the presence around her was growing stronger—could feel the weight of it pressing down on her as each day passed. And that evening, as she entered the building, it felt the heaviest. Emily had grown accustomed to it, had perfected her ability to ignore it. But since arriving in San Francisco, she found it more difficult to brush off the ominous spirit. She only hoped it stayed hidden from Liam. The thought of it latching onto and tormenting anyone around her was unbearable. She hoped it would lighten its grip on her soon. It was a cycle all too familiar to her. During any significant life change, the spirit made itself known by overshadowing her, as if to prove who was truly in charge.

Only this time, the presence felt more powerful than in the past. Consuming her thoughts and her dreams. "But it's open now. I saw it swinging open from outside."

"Would you like me to take a look?"

"You don't mind?" Emily asked.

"Of course not. It's part of my job description here," Liam said casually. He gestured with his hand toward Emily's door, "After you," and she led him inside.

Emily held her door open, inviting Liam into her flat. She hung her sweater and purse on the hook in the entry, and Liam waited in the middle of her living room. When she turned to face him, he asked, "So, how do you like the place?"

"I love it. The neighborhood is great. And it's quiet." A breeze blew through, causing Emily to shiver.

Liam turned to the window. "So this window here?"

"Yes. I have no idea why it keeps opening."

Liam pulled the window in, closing off the outside elements, and swung the latch to lock it before giving it a good push. "A breeze shouldn't be able to open it. It fits tight against the frame with the latch in place. It should be impossible for wind to catch it and swing it open. You said it's been happening a lot?"

Emily shivered once more. Instinct told her it wasn't a breeze causing the window to open, and her concern grew at the realization. The haunting had never manipulated her space before. Only making itself known by its presence and in her dreams. "Yes. Almost daily."

Liam bobbed his head as she spoke, still observing the window. "That is strange. I'll tell you what. I'll go grab a couple more latches and install them for you. That should keep it closed."

Emily stood staring at the window while Liam spoke. An eerie feeling washed over her, setting her on edge. Her skin pebbled as her hairs stood on end. Attempting again to ignore her reality of being haunted, she told herself it was just from the fog that had rolled in. It easily weaved itself into any void, bringing with it a drizzle that covered everything and could chill anyone to the bone.

"Everything okay?"

Emily jumped. She'd been unaware that she'd drifted off in her thoughts. "Huh? I'm sorry, what?"

"Is everything okay?"

"Oh, yes. I just got cold all of a sudden. Must be a draft from the open window. I'll just turn on the heat." She crossed to the opposite wall and switched on the thermostat, but nothing happened. No clicking or humming sounds from the vent, indicating that the furnace was working. "That's weird."

"What is?" Liam remained staring at the window.

"I don't hear the furnace kicking on."

"That is strange," he said as he turned. His crystal blue eyes met hers, and for a split second, she felt the urge to go to his side, to take his hand in hers, but she refrained. "I'll go down and take a look."

"Are you sure? You don't have to check right now. If you have things you need to do, I can wait."

"No. It's not a problem at all. Like I said, it's part of my job. I help Phil keep this place up. Plus, it's supposed to get pretty cold. It may be springtime, but it still gets cold here on the coast at night. I don't want you going without any heat. I'll be right back."

Emily felt more chilled by the minute and decided it was a good idea to let him take a look. "Okay. I really appreciate it."

"It's not a problem," Liam told her as he headed out of her front door and down the long, narrow hallway of the building.

Emily was now standing alone in her flat, yet she didn't feel alone. A disturbing sensation pricked her skin. Sinister, unseen, cold eyes watched her. A chill shook her again as she closed her front door, its icy grip closing in, suffocating her. "Go away," her voice wobbled. It gripped onto her soul tighter. "Leave me alone." She felt the entity release her, allowing her to take a lung full of air. She could breathe freely. For now.

***

Liam ran down the steps to the basement, his heart raced, and his breathing erratic. His rational mind told him it was impossible. He had never met her before. And if he ever had, he was sure he would have remembered. He could never forget her face. He'd been seeing it in his dreams for years.

He clasped his hands and brought them up to his mouth. His thoughts raced. She was beyond beautiful. Liam had been around beautiful women his entire life, but Emily captivated him. The pull he felt toward her was a powerful tethering sensation. As if invisible strings were reaching out and trying desperately to connect. The moment she turned and noticed him walking down the stairs, Liam's eyes caught hers, and his heart almost stopped.

She was average height, and he towered over her. He knew her head would fit comfortably on his chest under his chin in an embrace. The fantasy washed over him, bringing with it a rush of images from his dreams.

Everything about her was familiar to him. Freckles sprinkled across her nose and cheeks, while golden bronze ringlets fell loosely around her face and shoulders. A part of him knew how it would feel tangled in his hands. Her eyes were a warm brown, like dark wildflower honey. He wanted to fall into them and knew that in the right light, flecks of gold within them danced in the warm glow.

After taking a few moments to gather himself, he rubbed his hands through his hair. "One thing at a time," he whispered. His thoughts raced, but he forced himself to focus on his current task at hand.

He walked to the furnace. The thing was ancient. Of course it was. Phil always preferred to repair things rather than replace them. Even when Liam insisted that an appliance needed to be replaced, Phil put up a fight. Liam always chalked up the man's stubbornness to being old, stuck in his ways. The furnace wasn't original to the house, but it might as well have been. He was sure they didn't even make replacement parts for the thing anymore.

He noticed the pilot light was out. Of course he didn't have anything to relight it with him. Liam turned toward the steps to head upstairs. As he rounded the corner, something caught his attention—a glimpse of a shadow. It happened so quickly, he couldn't be sure exactly what it was. "Hello?" he called out. "Is anyone down here?" But who would be in the basement? The lower level apartment was unoccupied. It always had been. In fact, Liam had never been inside the apartment. Phil said it was too run down, and he was using it for storage.

Liam walked back to the furnace, a natural reaction he had fine-tuned in his line of work over the years. Never leave a stone unturned. But there was nothing there. No one was in sight, and he could see if anyone was down there with him as there was nowhere to hide. The wooden staircase was the only access to the basement.

An uneasiness came over him, the same foreboding feeling from a few minutes earlier when he stepped away from Emily's window. It was a queasiness in his stomach that always warned him something was about to happen. He had lived in that house for years, and nothing unexplainable had ever taken place. Still, Liam couldn't shake his instinct, alerting him that something was amiss. Not sure what to make of what he'd just experienced, Liam headed back upstairs to his flat and grabbed a butane lighter. On his way back to the basement, his thoughts, once again, drifted to Emily and the look of worry on her face.

He was certain her startled reaction was in response to more than just a chill in the air and wondered if she recognized him the way he recognized her. When Liam had turned away from the window, he noticed she was distracted and a little on edge. She jumped when he spoke, and her unease was evident. He had seen that look before but didn't dare say anything. She was spooked, and the last thing Liam wanted to do was cause her any more alarm. He had to fight the instinct to run to her. The need to wrap his arms around her was overwhelming. He always had control over his emotions, but for whatever reason, the need to care for this woman's well-being overtook him.

The warm feeling that rushed over him when he entered her flat took him by surprise. He had been inside a few times to make repairs for past occupants, with the most recent being when he repainted the walls after the previous tenant moved out. Liam took in the charming, homey feel of her flat. It was girlie, soft, and delicate, but sophisticated. Her sofa was a neutral cream tone, as was most of her furniture, but she accented the space with bits of color in soft shades that welcomed you in.

For a moment, Liam pictured himself lounging on her sofa, drinking a beer while having a conversation with her. He had no idea where that thought had come from. He blinked, pulling himself back to the present before he crossed her living room to examine her window.

Liam rounded the corner of the basement stairs once more, and the dreadful feeling from a few minutes ago had grown in intensity. He cautiously made his way toward the furnace. When he knelt to examine the pilot light, he gasped before falling back. His heart hammered, and he felt himself go pale. "What the fuck?" he whispered. Liam knew it had been out. How could it be lit now?

Liam rubbed his hands across his face and surveyed the basement again, making sure there was absolutely no one down there who could be fooling around. Crossing to the apartment door across from the furnace, he checked that the padlock was still there. It was locked from the outside, making it impossible for anyone to be hiding on the other side of the door.

Baffled, Liam wasn't sure what to think. His mind moved a hundred miles a minute with potential theories. Needing to get to a place where he could think clearly, he hurried up the stairs to Emily's flat. As he reached the top of the stairs, the furnace kicked on and heated, as if it were good as new.

Liam pulled in three long, deep breaths to steady himself before knocking on Emily's door. When she opened the door, and her angelic face came in to view, he willed his heart to stop pounding.

"Hey, thanks! Whatever you did worked. The furnace just came on."

"You're welcome. It was just the pilot light. If anything else happens, let me know right away. No matter the time. Okay?"

"Okay." Emily paused, her lips slightly parted as if she were going to say something.

"Well, it was good to meet you, Emily." Liam wanted to reach out and touch her. Stroke her hair, caress her cheek. He tamped down the feeling. His senses were an erratic mess, and he needed to pull his head together.

"It was good to meet you too, Liam. Thanks again."

"You're welcome. Don't hesitate to let me know if you need anything. I'll be back in the morning to install those extra latches on the window. Ten o'clock okay?"

"Yes. That will be fine. I'll be here. I'll see you tomorrow." Emily smiled, and Liam caught the gold flecks that he remembered from his dream shimmer in her brown eyes.

"Good. I'll see you in the morning. Have a good night." Liam watched as Emily closed her door. He stood in the hallway for a minute, collecting himself. Needing fresh air and to clear his head, he decided to walk to the hardware store.

Outside, he stood in the front of the old building and glanced up toward Emily's window. It was still closed. A part of him hoped he would glimpse her peering out. But her curtains remained drawn. Only the soft glow of her lights shone through. Liam's heart raced. The woman he'd dreamt about for years was real, and she was living in the flat below his. A moment later, his stomach twisted, a feeling of anxiousness overtook him. Something was going on. He was sure of it. He just needed to figure out what.

Three

Emily woke feeling more exhausted than she did when she had gone to bed. Her sleep had been inundated with vivid nightmares that woke her throughout the night. She had dealt with terrible dreams for as long as she could remember. But lately, they were more frequent, and she couldn't put her finger as to what the cause may be. This morning, she wanted nothing more than to bury her aching head under the covers and sleep the day away. She whimpered softly to herself, knowing that was not going to be an option.

With her head pounding, she rolled to the side, and using only one eye to squint at her phone, she saw it was 7:30. That gave her a couple hours to get ready, put herself together, and nurse her headache. She had work to do on her new website for her photography business. Since she lived in a new city, she needed to update her site and social media pages to make her online presence known to the local community. Plus, Liam was supposed to be coming by to fix her living room window.

She needed to get up. But first, she snatched her phone from the nightstand to respond to her friend, Lexi. In typical Lexi style, she had sent Emily a text message first thing in the morning. The two of them had been friends for forever. They considered themselves sisters and texted with each other all day, every day. Only lately, it had been less frequent with Lexi being busier than usual at her job and Emily's recent move.

Lexi: What's up, woman? It's Saturday. You have any plans today?

Emily: Not really. I may go for a walk later. Maybe find a coffee shop and get some work done. You?

A few moments passed, and Lexi responded with…

Lexi: Claire called in sick. Again. So I'm at the hotel covering for her.

Emily: Again? What's up with her?

Lexi: No idea. I'm tired of it though. I need a change.

Emily: Move down here?

Lexi: I'll work on it.

Emily: I gotta get ready. TTYL

Lexi's response was a ridiculous amount of emojis of hearts, smiley, and kissy faces. Followed by **XOXOXO's,** and **I miss you**.

Emily smiled before moving to the edge of the bed, where she gently stretched her neck and padded her way to the bathroom. She grabbed some Ibuprofen from the medicine cabinet, cupped her hands under the sinks faucet, and swallowed the medicine.

Emily looked in the mirror and was startled by her reflection. The circles under her eyes looked more like bruises than the typical light shadows she normally had after a bad night of sleep. Her complexion appeared sallow. It would be a makeup kind of day for sure.

The sound of floorboards creaking caught her attention. It sounded as if someone were walking. Peeking her head out into the hallway, she had a clear view of most of her apartment. No one was there. And she spotted the chain lock on her door still in place. It was probably Liam walking around upstairs. The building was old. Emily had read that the majority of the Victorian homes in San Francisco had been built in the mid-eighteen hundreds. The house was well over a hundred and fifty years old and bound to come with creaking and settling sounds.

Stepping into the shower, Emily stood under the spray of the hot water, letting it cascade over her. Her mind drifted to her new neighbor, Liam. She couldn't help but notice how attractive he was when she met him last night. In the past, Emily had never been attracted to men with facial hair, but on Liam, she thought it was sexy as hell.

It had been years since Emily had dated, and she hoped that starting her new life in a new city would be the spark she needed to live a normal life. Her last boyfriend had been a disaster, and she swore off dating forever at the time. But after seeing Liam last night, dating kind of made its way back into the forefront of her mind. He was tall, incredibly gorgeous, kind of mysterious too. That was new for her. But maybe, she needed new and different. Hell, that was why she left Seattle in the first place. She wanted a change. The spontaneous pull she felt to move ignited a desire within her to live a life she had always wanted. To find peace and be happy. Maybe even find love.

She shook the thought from her head. What were the chances that Liam was even available? Knowing her luck, he probably had a gorgeous girlfriend. Emily had never thought of herself as being particularly attractive. The thought that someone like Liam could be attracted to her was far-fetched in her mind.

Maybe she would just let things play out and see what would come of it. If she had learned anything through her trials in life, it was never to get her hopes up. Staying neutral was safe, and if she got more than she thought she would, great! If not, no harm done. That was how she lived her life. Completely neutral.

Clearing the thoughts of Liam from her mind, Emily mulled over ideas for her website. It was early spring and considered to be the offseason still. There wasn't much work for photographers just yet. Most people who were getting married that summer would have already hired their photographers. So, she decided that focusing on family photo sessions for the summer was her best bet. Next year she would have plenty of weddings to photograph.

With her head still under the running water, she felt the hairs on her arms and the back of her neck stand up, and a cold breeze blew past her. She knew all of the windows in her flat were closed and could hear the faint hum of the furnace running through the vent. Perhaps the living room window blew open again? But she closed the bathroom door, so how could the breeze come through?

The air changed. Electricity swirled, prickling Emily's skin with pins and needles. Goosebumps formed, inflaming her body with tiny, painfully hard lumps. Her breathing quickened, and her heart hammered against her ribs. Despite the cold blowing around her, her face flushed, and her ears rang. Afraid she might pass out, Emily pressed her back against the cold tile behind her.

Another bitter cold breeze blew through. This time, Emily could see her breath in the chilled air. She lifted her gaze and turned her head. Looking through the opaque, white shower curtain, a shadow stood near the door. Emily sucked in a breath of air, where it froze in her lungs. Unable to move, she stared at the form in front of her. It was hard to make out what it was exactly. It resembled a human form—one of a man with broad shoulders and much taller than her. Only it did not look natural. It pulsated, becoming more solid before fading and coming back into view—a void of darkness against the light in the room.

"Hello?" was all Emily could manage. Fear rose within her. She turned off the water, hoping the absence of the sound would clear her hearing. It did, but only barely. Her ears still rung from the fluctuating energy swirling around her, and a funhouse effect took over her equilibrium. Her balance was off, and her legs wobbled. She hesitantly reached for the shower curtain. Not wanting to look, but knowing she had to see what had invaded her space.

Gripping the edge of the curtain, she mustered all of her courage to pull it back. Only she didn't have to. In an instant, whatever was in her bathroom lunged toward her, stopping inches away from the other side of the curtain. She could now clearly see the shadowy outline of a person. Complete blackness in the form of a man stood in front of her. Watching her on the other side of her shower.

The hair-raising scream that escaped her throat pierced her own ears. Shutting her eyes, she crouched into a protective ball before another icy blast of air shot through her. She shivered uncontrollably now, from fear, the cold, and the sudden rush of adrenaline.

After a moment, she dared to look up. When there was no sight of the figure, she stood on shaky legs and once again reached for the shower curtain. Slowly pulling it open, she looked around and breathed a sigh of relief when it was evident nothing was standing in her bathroom.

Swallowing hard and stepping out of the shower, Emily grabbed a towel and dried herself. An unexpected knock at the door caused her to gasp and jump. With adrenaline still pulsing through her, it took a second for her to realize what she was hearing.

"Emily?" It sounded like Liam. She recognized his smooth tone. Why was he here so early? He said ten o'clock. It was just now eight, and she was in no condition to open the door at the moment. He must have heard her scream.

Another knock. "Emily? Are you in there?" He sounded worried.

Emily toweled off as quickly as she could manage. With her hands still shaking, she grabbed her plush, pink robe hanging on the hook on the bathroom door, and threw it on.

"I'm coming," she said as she hurried down the hallway.

When she unlatched the chain and turned the deadbolt, she

cracked the door open. Liam stood in sweats and a t-shirt, the concern on his face apparent. "Are you okay?"

"Yes. I-I-I'm okay," Emily answered, in a failed attempt at using a steady voice.

"Are you sure? Why did you scream?"

Emily felt the blood leave her face at the memory of what she had just seen. She gripped the doorknob so tight, her knuckles went white as she willed herself not to pass out. "I thought I saw something. That's all."

Liam stepped ever so slightly toward her and lowered his tone. "I don't want to overstep my boundaries, but you're shaking and pale. Did something happen? Can I come in?"

Emily thought for a second. It was obvious he was worried, and he had told her to let him know if anything else happened. "Okay. Come in." She opened the door and allowed him to step inside. "Can you give me a minute?"

"Of course," he responded. Emily turned and headed down the small hallway to her bedroom and closed the door behind her. She opened multiple drawers at her dresser and pulled out a pair of underwear, her favorite leggings, a bra, and an oversized hoodie.

She got dressed, then grabbed a scrunchie off of her nightstand, and put her hair in a messy bun on top of her head. She would deal with the tangled mess later. When she made her way back to the living room, Liam was standing at the window, inspecting it.

"I didn't mean to alarm you. I was just startled—"

Liam put up his hand to stop her. "Emily, it's okay. Obviously, something scared the crap out of you. Can we sit? I'd like to hear about what startled you."

Emily wanted to sit. Her legs still felt like Jell-O as if she had just run a marathon. She gave a silent nod and took a seat on the sofa. Liam joined her, and she noticed a subtle, spicy scent emanating off of him.

Sitting with his body facing her, she was surprised at the amount of concern he was showing. "Can I ask why you're so concerned? Don't get me wrong, I'm glad there's a familiar face here right now, but why are you so interested in what I saw?"

Liam stared at Emily intensely before answering. "Because I have a feeling I know what you saw."

Emily didn't think she could turn anymore pale, but the sensation of more blood leaving her face proved her wrong. "What do you mean?"

"I'm a paranormal investigator. That's why I travel so much. I've seen people scared the way you are right now. I've also seen something recently. In the basement, last night." Liam took a deep breath. "I thought I saw a figure down there. As I was coming back upstairs to get a lighter to relight the pilot, something caught my attention, but then it was gone. And when I went back down there, the pilot light was relit, on its own."

Bringing her knees to her chest, Emily wrapped her arms around her legs and hugged herself in an attempt to calm the quaking that was taking over her body. "Emily, please tell me what you saw. I need to know if something is going on here. Because if something *is* going on here, my friends and I can help."

Not wanting to remember the image she had seen through her shower curtain, but still feeling a sense of urgency to confide in Liam, Emily met his gaze. "You're a paranormal investigator?"

That's convenient. Emily thought. Maybe her prayers had finally been answered. Perhaps the universe was working in her favor, leading her to a place where she could find someone to confide in. Someone who she could tell all of her past experiences to. Someone who wouldn't think she was mentally unstable.

"Yes. I am," Liam nodded.

Emily could not believe what she was about to share with her new neighbor. But there was no going back now. She had made up her mind, and she could only hope that he wouldn't think she was crazy.

"I saw a shadow. While I was in the shower."

"Go on..." he told her.

"It got really cold. So cold, I could see my breath, even with all the hot water. My hearing went funny. I thought I was going to pass out. It kept getting colder, and when I turned, there was a shadow of a man standing on the other side of my shower curtain, near the door. I couldn't see a face. It was solid, black, in the outline of a man. Then, it rushed toward me. It came up to the shower. It was just blackness. That's when I screamed, and it was gone."

Liam didn't seem to be fazed by Emily's explanation, and her heart calmed. A glimmer of hope sparked within her, raising her confidence that Liam could be trusted. He sat and nodded his head when she finished speaking.

"Okay. We will figure out what is going on here. I'm going to call Phil and see if anything like this has ever happened before. I'm also going to call my team and let them know what has happened and see what we can come up with. Are you okay with me telling them what you saw?"

Emily's throat was stuck. Emotion collecting into a tight knot, she found it difficult to find her voice. She only nodded her head to let him know that she understood what he was saying. "Are you going to be okay if I go back upstairs and make some calls? If anything happens, just come upstairs and bang on the door. Hell, you can even yell or scream for me. I'll hear you."

"I think I'll be okay," Emily managed a smile. "I woke up with a terrible headache. I'm going to lay right here and watch some TV."

"Alright. I'll come back and tell you what I find out from Phil in a little bit."

Liam stood and took Emily's hand, helping her stand up. "Lock the door behind me," he told her.

She did and made her way back to the sofa, where she plopped down and pulled a blanket over herself. Emily grabbed the remote and flipped through the channels until she found the weekend morning news. She tried to settle herself and relax. But it was no use. Her anxiety was too high. She needed to talk. She needed her best friend.

Grabbing her phone, she swiped it open and called Lexi. Relief swept over her when Lexi answered. She briefly explained the morning's phenomenon. "He's a paranormal investigator?" Lexi screeched into the phone so loudly, Emily had to pull it away from her ear. "Em, you have to tell him! I know you think he's going to think you're insane, but he won't. He shouldn't. If he's any good at what he does for a living, he'll want to help you and not pass judgment."

Emily knew Lexi was asking her not to compare Liam to Ben, a psychologist who she dated briefly a few years back. Emily thought that since Ben had been a psychologist, she could confide in him and tell him what she had been experiencing her entire life. Boy, was she wrong. Instead of comforting her and offering to help her figure out what was happening around her, he basically made her feel like a nut case and tried to get her to take prescription anti-anxiety meds. She ended the relationship shortly after his insistence that she be on medication. He was the only other person, aside from Lexi, who Emily tried to explain what had been haunting her. She knew Lexi was right. Liam was not Ben. Maybe he would be able to help.

"I know, Lex. It's just hard. I don't want to scare him away."

"You like him?"

Emily grabbed the remote and began flipping channels again. "If you're asking if he's a nice person and polite, then the answer is yes."

"Is he hot?"

Emily threw her head back against the sofa, huffing out a breath in frustration. "Lexi!" she yelled at her friend's assumption.

"What? You've been living there for a couple weeks. You guys have talked a bunch. What's the big deal if you notice he's attractive or not? Ghostly stuff aside, if you like him, see if he's available."

"We only just met. Last night, Lex. We've had two conversations, Lexi. Two. One of those two was after I'd come face to face with a fucking ghost and could barely stand or speak because I was shaking so badly. So what if he's attractive? He'll probably still think I'm a basket case. Who wants to date a person who's had a ghost following her practically her entire life?"

"A paranormal investigator, that's who! Em, you need to go after that."

"Alexis, drop it." Emily knew her friend meant well, but she was exhausted and the Ibuprofen she had taken did not seem to be working.

"Okay, okay. But hey. I'll make you a bet. I bet he asks you out in the next week. It's obvious he likes you. If he didn't, he wouldn't have run down stairs to check on you or insist that he come in to talk to you about what you saw. Just saying."

Emily thought about Lexi's statement. She was right. But she just couldn't bring herself to think about that at the moment. "Bye, Lex. I'll call you tonight and let you know how things go today."

"Okay, hon. Try not to worry. Don't forget to call. You know I'll worry myself sick if you do. I'll talk to you later."

They both hung up. Emily felt relieved after talking to her friend. Aside from her relentless attempt at getting her to hook up with Liam, she knew Lexi only had her best interest in mind.

Closing her eyes and willing her head to stop pounding, she barely registered the conversation between the news anchors on the morning news program. Emily pulled the blanket to her chin, cocooning herself into a ball, and fell asleep.

Four

Holy shit! Liam's mind combed through possible explanations on what could have started a haunting in the home. Liam's heart hammered in his chest. Nothing along any paranormal lines had ever happened in the five years he lived in the building. Why now? What was going on?

Emily's confirmation that she had seen a shadow both relieved and mystified him. It confirmed that there actually was something lurking in the basement the night before. But why? And who or what was the shadow?

He needed to call Phil. Maybe he had information on the history of the house. He would also inform his fellow investigators, Trey and Luke, on what was going on. They would help dig up information about the property that could explain the strange and sudden haunting.

Liam walked through his flat, contemplating pouring himself a drink. As much as he wanted to, he quickly decided against the idea as it was just too early. He would wait until he saw his friends later that day.

Pulling his phone out of his pocket, he sent a group text message to his teammates.

Liam: Trey, I need a favor. Remember I told you about the

woman who moved in downstairs? There's been some weird shit happening. Something's going on here in the house.

Trey: What's up?

Liam: Too much to type. I need you to see if you can come up with anything on the history of this house. You're better at this shit than I am. And the sooner, the better if you can swing it.

Trey was Liam's right-hand man. He wasn't only his friend but also his teammate and fellow co-founder of their paranormal investigation company. He'd always been able to rely on Trey for anything. They'd known each other since elementary school, and they were as close as brothers.

And then there was Luke, who Liam and Trey had met during high school. He was their tech guy and maintained all of the equipment for the team. The three of them started investigating together during their senior year of high school. Trey was a history buff and was in charge of all the research when they did an investigation. Liam was a paranormal enthusiast, and he'd been infatuated with anything that had to do with ghosts and hauntings since he was a boy. Luke kept up to date on all of the latest investigation technology and even worked closely with a friend, who was a scientist and help develop new ghost hunting tools.

One day, while watching a ghost investigation show on TV together, they came up with the idea of starting their own investigation business. They called themselves The Spirit Hunters and traveled together after graduating high school, investigating the paranormal in different locations throughout the country.

They mostly dealt with large locations that had historical significance, like old hotels, abandoned hospitals, and prisons. Every now and then, they would receive a call from a residential location. Those were the calls that were always made the team's number one priority.

As he was scrolling through his contacts to pull up Phil's number, a text came through with Trey's response.

Trey: No problem. I'll get right on it. Off the top of my head, because I know you're wondering, I can't think of any crazy stuff that ever happened in that neck of the woods. But I'll see if I can pull up any public records on the place. Maybe something happened that never hit the news. Has anything significant happened since you talked to us last night?

Not wanting to go into too much detail through text, Liam responded with:

Liam: Thanks. Appreciate it. I'd really rather sit down and talk to you two in person. What are you doing today? Can you meet me at the Cliff House in an hour?

His phone chimed.

Luke: I'll be there, brother.

Trey: See you in a bit.

Closing the text app and going back into his contacts, Liam found Phil's number and pressed the call button. It rang with no answer, only sending him to voicemail. Of course, when he needed information, the old man didn't answer. After cursing, he composed himself and left Phil a message saying that he needed him to call him back as soon as possible. It had to do with the house, and he needed information.

In the bathroom, he picked up his electric beard trimmer and ran it along his facial hair. He preferred the mustache and beard but kept them closely shaved. He caught his reflection in the mirror and was taken back to the night before. When he had first seen Emily, his breath caught in his chest. At first, he chalked it all up to her beauty. Her golden-brown eyes were captivating. He wanted to reach out and caress her ivory skin. A part of him knew how silky it would feel under his fingertips. The thought of running his fingers through her dark brown locks of hair swept through his mind. There had been an overwhelming feeling that he was seeing a long lost friend and not just meeting someone for the first time.

As busy as he had been traveling, he had not really noticed women lately. In fact, the concept of dating hadn't entered his mind in quite some time. He had convinced himself the night before that was the reason he felt drawn to her.

But after seeing Emily this morning, there was no doubt in his mind as to who she was. It wasn't just her beauty. Though she was absolutely breathtaking. It was her presence, her energy. Her soft, sultry voice…

Shaking his head, Liam jumped in the shower and continued to get ready. Before leaving his flat, he checked his phone again, but there was still no response from Phil, so he sent a text to the team, letting them know he was leaving. Once on the main level of the house, he knocked on Emily's door softly so as not to startle her. He worried he'd woken her because she looked groggy when she answered the door. "Hey," Liam said. "I have to head out and talk to my team. I called Phil, but he didn't pick up, so I left him a message to call me back."

"Okay."

"Will you be alright alone? I can have the guys meet me here, so you're not alone in the building."

Emily smiled and let out a sexy giggle. "Yes. I'll be fine. Go, see your friends. Don't worry. I can take care of myself." Emily's smile turned into a grin, revealing a dimple on her cheek, just below her left eye.

"I'm positive you can. I just wanted to be sure." Liam reached in his back pocket, pulled out a business card from his wallet, and handed it to Emily. "Here. My cell number is on there. If anything happens, anything at all, you call me. Okay?"

Emily's hand lightly brushed his as she took the business card, and he felt an electrical current shoot through his arm. It was the same pulsing sensation he felt last night when he had shaken her hand, and again a little while earlier when he helped her off of the sofa. He wasn't sure if Emily had felt the same sensation. She stared at the card. Her thumb caressed the ink on the paper, making it hard for him to read her face. A part of him hoped she'd felt something.

"Thank you, Liam."

Emily looked up and met his eyes. They were the most magnificent whisky brown color he had ever seen. "I'll let you know when I get back. Can I bring you anything? Some lunch?"

"Oh, you don't have to." Emily shook her head while she spoke.

Something sparked in Liam. He needed to come back anyway and install the latches on her window, and for reasons unknown to him, her well-being was now his top priority. "It's not a problem. My treat. As a belated housewarming gift. It's the least I can do after the kind of morning you had. I'll let you get some rest. When I get back, I'll install those latches for you too."

"That's sweet of you. Thank you."

"Rest up. I'll see you in a bit."

Liam took a step away from her door as she closed it, and he waited to hear the sound of the deadbolt engaging. He waited for a beat before heading out of the building. Outside, Liam paused, taking a cleansing breath. If he wasn't one hundred percent sure who she was a few minutes ago, there was no doubt in his mind about who she was now.

"My god," he said to himself. He needed to get to his team. Fast.

Five

The wind blew more forcefully than usual. The waves crashed violently against the rocky shore, sending a salty spray into the air, colliding with the foggy mist that kissed the coastline. The robust scent of damp earth and pavement was magnified by the morning fog that had not yet retreated back, and sprinkled droplets coated everything in cold dampness. Dark overcast skies blanketed the city, indicating that heavier rain was on the way. Despite that, the natural beauty of the landscape and Mother Nature coming together created a picturesque scene.

Liam sat at a table by a window watching the waves break. He had ordered a drink and waited for Trey and Luke to arrive. Emily had told him that it was okay if he shared her paranormal experience from that morning, and Liam was glad she trusted him and his friends to help them get to the bottom of the situation.

Liam had reservations about leaving Emily alone. But her insistence that she would be fine eased his anxiety, and she now had his phone number. And, he hoped she wouldn't hesitate to use it.

He requested a table in the back corner of the restaurant to ensure privacy. While waiting for his friends, his mind relentlessly turned over theories in a desperate attempt to find answers to what was happening. Under normal circumstances, a new case would excite him. He would relish in the opportunity to sink his teeth into a new case and gather new evidence of paranormal activity. Adding the investigation to the ever-growing cases of unexplainable phenomenon while trying to develop solutions for the anomaly victims.

However, the case with Emily had his stomach wrenching with uncertain apprehension. Why had the activity begun as soon as she arrived? And why was she so familiar to him? What was the shadow figure?

The moment Liam made eye contact with her last night, electricity shot through him. He instantly knew who she was. But at the same time, he was certain he had never met her before. How could she be real? She only lived in his dreams. It was as if a forgotten memory of her was floating beneath the surface, blurry at the edges, becoming more defined as he dove deeper.

"Hey, Liam. Snap out of it."

Startled, he looked up. Having been so lost in his thoughts, he had not noticed Trey and Luke walk up to the table. "Hey. Sorry, guys. It's been a morning."

"Seems like it," Trey said while he and Luke took their seat. "What the hell is going on. I've never seen this look on you before. You're worried. Spill it."

If there was anyone Liam could trust, it was Trey and Luke. He was not so much afraid about telling them what was going on as he was finding out what was *really* going on.

After the waitress jotted down their breakfast orders, the three of them talked for about an hour. Liam explained in more detail what he had seen while working on the furnace the night before. He also told them about Emily's window being open, as well as her story about the shadow figure in her bathroom. That was when Luke spoke, "Where is she now? From how you described what happened, it sounds like she's pretty freaked out. Is she okay?"

"I talked to her before coming here. She insisted she's fine. I gave her my number, told her not to hesitate to call if anything happens." Liam rubbed his hands down his face, clasping them together under his chin, and resting his elbows on the table. "I have a feeling she's not sharing everything with me, though. I need to talk to her more. She's definitely leaving out some details."

He took a sip of his vodka and cranberry, deciding at the last moment to down the rest of it. The stares from his friends were palpable.

"Liam, what is it? There's something *you're* not telling us."

Liam was the leader of the team. The levelheaded, calm force that held everyone together in stressful situations. Now, he was a shaky ball of nerves with a case that he had no idea how to tackle.

Inhaling deeply and deciding that he should not keep his teammates in the dark, Liam leaned further over the table and lowered his voice to a soft tone. "I'm almost positive that she's *the* woman from my dream."

Trey and Luke sat silent for a heartbeat before saying at the same time, "You mean, *the woman?*"

"Yeah. It's her. Only it's present-day now. But I knew it the moment I saw her. I haven't wanted to believe it. Told myself it's just a coincidence. But when I saw her again this morning after I heard her scream, and again right before I left to come here, there's no doubt in my mind that it's her."

Luke sat back in his chair. "Wow."

Liam sat back. Now that he'd gotten that information off his chest, he felt more relaxed. "I barely slept last night, and when I did sleep, I dreamt of her again. I feel this strong pull toward her." Liam balled his fist and pressed it to the center of his chest. "It's hard to explain. When I first saw her, it was like something shot through me and anchored into my chest."

"So you think cupid shot his arrow at you?" Luke chimed in.

Annoyed, but understanding his friend's sense of humor, Liam replied, "No dipshit. Not cupid. It's deeper than that."

"Does she have this same feeling? Did you tell her?" Trey asked.

"Hell no! I haven't said anything yet. How can I? I don't want to scare her any more than I know she already is. I'm practically a stranger to her."

Luke looked at his friend and grinned from ear to ear. "Oh, dude. You've got it bad."

Trey spoke again, "Liam, you've gotta tell her. Don't you think it's strange that there's never been any kind of paranormal activity in that house since you've been living there? Then, all of a sudden, one day, a woman, who you've been dreaming about for over a decade, moves in, and activity starts? That's not a coincidence. You know that as much as we do. Something is going on that involves the two of you. You need to tell her. You said you feel like she's not telling you everything. Maybe she's hiding some detail and is scared to tell you. Maybe she's dreaming of you too. Talk to her."

Liam stared down at his empty glass, swirling the leftover ice cubes, watching them mingle with the drops of liquid at the bottom. "Trust me. You're not telling me anything that I haven't already thought of. I'm going to talk to her. I already told her that I'm a paranormal investigator. She actually seems intrigued. I'm just not sure how to tell her that I've been seeing her in my dreams for the last fifteen years."

Everyone remained quiet. Liam knew Trey was right. He also knew he was going to stick to his gut instinct and wait for an opportune time to fill Emily in on the details of his dreams.

"She's pretty freaked out. Quite frankly, so am I. I called Phil to see if he could give me a rundown on the history of the building. But he didn't answer and hasn't called me back yet. I thought about waiting until after I talk to him to see if he has any information that could help before we do an investigation. But you know what? Fuck it. We can't wait. He's not the one here dealing with whatever this is and seeing shadow figures. Emily and I are."

The men were silent but nodded their approvals.

"He won't know the difference. I say we do an investigation and find out what the hell is going on. Are you guys up for it?"

Both men looked at him. "Oh, hell yeah! You know we're with you, brother," Trey said.

"Dude, you don't even have to ask. You know I'm in," Luke agreed.

Six

Liam returned home with food. He didn't know if there was anything Emily wouldn't or couldn't eat, but he assumed there wasn't since she hadn't specified anything when she excepted his offer to bring her something to eat.

Liam wasn't sure what was going on with his head. All he knew was that the thought of Emily both comforted and made him nervous at the same time, twisting his gut into a ball of anxiety that he wasn't sure he wanted relief from.

His nerves were wound tight when he arrived back at the house. After grabbing a few tools from his flat upstairs and giving himself a pep talk about being relaxed and composed, he stopped in front of Emily's door. He lifted his hand to knock but hesitated. Shit! What the hell was wrong with him? Normally, he was pretty calm and confident. But this woman was messing with his mind in ways he never thought possible. It both captivated and scared the shit out of him.

Pulling in a deep breath, he knocked. Moments later, he heard the telltale sound of the lock being unlatched from the other side, and her door opened. "Hey!" he said before being frozen in amazement.

Emily was dressed in the same black leggings she had on when he left, but she had changed her sweatshirt to an oversized sweater. It was a dusty pink color and fell slightly off one shoulder, revealing the delicate bones under her neck. Although the sweater looked too big on her, it draped over her perfectly, revealing a hint of her curves. Her golden-brown hair was no longer in a bun on top of her head. It was now down and fell in loose waves around her face and shoulders. She wore just the slightest bit of makeup that accented her whiskey brown eyes and a hint of color on her high cheekbones. And her full lips were tinted in a soft pink with the slightest touch of gloss. His mouth watered at the sight of them.

Liam felt the need to walk toward her, lean in, and taste what flavor of gloss she had on. The thought of crashing his mouth on hers overtook his imagination, and he found himself blinking, forcing the fantasy from his mind.

"Hi!" her voice was low and dripped of sweetness.

"You look better. Did you get some rest?"

"Yes, I did."

"I brought you some food. Like I promised." He lifted the bag in his hand and caught the blush that crept up from her chest and spread up to her cheeks.

"That was so nice of you. Do you want to come in?"

Yes! he thought. "Sure. I have those latches for your window too. I'll install those while you eat."

"Okay." Emily opened the door fully and led him to the small galley kitchen just off of the intimate dining area. He set the food on the counter. "It smells wonderful."

"It's from one of my favorite restaurants. I hope you like it. I realized when I ordered it that I didn't ask you what you like to eat."

Emily looked at him and gently shook her head. "Oh, I am not picky." Her smile grew as she spoke.

"I'm glad to hear that. It's Cony Island-style clam chowder."

"Really?" Her brows pinched together slightly. Curiosity coated her tone. "I've never heard of such a thing."

"It's delicious," Liam assured her. "It's clam chowder only with a tomato base broth instead of the traditional cream base."

Emily opened the bag, pulled out the soup, then opened the container. The smell of the steaming liquid wafted through the kitchen. "It smells divine," she said while inhaling the delightful aroma. "What else is there?" she asked, her eyes brightened with wonder.

Liam couldn't help chuckling at her enthusiasm. "Just a sandwich, but just as tasty as the soup, I promise. It has ham and turkey and cheese. There's also the famous San Franciscan sourdough to go with the soup. I hope you like it."

"Oh, I'm sure I will. Thank you…so much," she said, turning to him.

"You're very welcome, Emily. Now eat. Don't mind me. I'm going to install these latches."

"You should eat too!"

Liam shook his head while grinning. "I ate with the guys. I'm good."

Emily watched as Liam installed the latches on her window. The heat of her stare on him caused his body to react, and he prayed he could relax and reverse the effect her attention had on him.

Not helping his situation, and not able to help himself, every time Liam would steal a glance in her direction, he hoped she wouldn't be looking his way. She sat cross-legged on her sofa with a magazine in her lap and ate a bowl of soup while dunking the hearty sourdough bread in the broth. And once again, he thought about what it would be like to kiss her full, luscious lips. Even though he had just eaten, a different kind of hunger crept up on him, and he was certain it was not for the soup.

Liam hurried to finish installing the latches on her window. Being in such close proximity to Emily was beginning to drive him mad, and he needed to pull his head together. When he secured the last latch, he walked to where she was sitting on the sofa. He initially had no intention of sitting down, but he turned and sat on a whim, angling his body. "Did anything happen while I was gone?" He put his arm over the back of the sofa. Emily placed her empty bowl on the coffee table in front of them and turned herself to look into his eyes.

"No. Nothing happened. Trust me. Had I seen that thing again, I would have called you."

"Good." Liam felt relief that Emily hadn't been disturbed by the anomaly while he was away. "I talked to my friends."

"I figured you had. What did they say?"

"Well, I explained to them what I'd seen and what you'd seen. We all agreed to do an investigation if that's all right with you."

"Yes, of course. Will we be able to find out what is going on?"

"Hopefully. We just need to gather as much information about the property as we can first. See if there's anything that might help us understand what we're dealing with. It might take a little time. We have some local cases that we're committed to. As soon as we get through those, we can focus more on this place."

Emily nodded. "I'll keep you up to date with what I find out. And I want you to tell me right away if anything else happens. You have my number handy?"

"Yes," she told him. "I put it in my phone already."

Liam's heart rate spiked at her declaration. Emily stared at him with questions in her eyes. He wanted to ask her what she was thinking, wanted to know what thoughts danced around in her head. Knowing he needed to earn her trust first, pushing her too fast for information could cause her to clam up and hold onto the secrets he knew she was keeping, he tamped down his own desire to know everything in that moment. He had no idea how he knew. A feeling deep within him clawed at the surface. His instincts screamed that there was more. So much more. Despite it all, Liam committed to himself that he would go slow and be patient.

The flecks of gold in her brown eyes glistened, and he became lost in them for a moment. Not really knowing how to hold back, the words escaped his lips, "What are you doing tomorrow?"

Emily blinked in surprise. Had she been daydreaming about him too? The light flush of rosiness that spread across her chest and face told him all he needed to know.

"I—" she hesitated.

In an attempt to calm her nerves, he added, "I was wondering if you'd like to have a tour of the city."

Emily's lips curled up on one side. She tilted her head slightly, "Are you asking me on a date?"

"I am," he told her firmly.

"You're not already taken?"

"No. I'm single. I haven't dated anyone in a long time."

Emily inhaled, and then exhaled. "Oh."

"Did you think I was dating someone?" Liam asked her.

"Honestly, I figured there was no way you weren't dating anyone. You're really attractive and incredibly kind. I'm actually a little surprised you're single."

Liam smiled wide at her compliment. It wasn't lost on him that he was good looking. He knew women were drawn to him. He'd seen women trip over their own feet in an attempt to scramble over to him whenever he went out with Trey and Luke. But the truth was, he was never into dating women just for the fun of it. He'd had a couple of serious relationships throughout the years, and he had cared for the women he had dated. But nothing ever came of the relationships with them. There was never a deep connection. One in which he believed only true soulmates could share.

His parents always said they were soulmates, that there was no one else on Earth meant for them. That's what Liam was waiting for. For the one person who knew every inch of his soul, and whose he knew in return.

Emily's lips parted as if she were about to speak, but nothing escaped them at first. After a beat, she nodded and said, "I would really like that."

Relief swept over him. The breath he had been holding escaped in a whoosh, and he caught Emily smiling at him. Her smile was warm, kind, and genuine. "Okay, then. Can I come by here around eleven?"

"Eleven is perfect."

Standing, Liam held out his hand to help Emily off of the sofa, and he felt a subtle tremble when their skin touched. He held her hand the entire eight and a half steps to the door. Yes, he counted them and savored every moment.

"I'll be right upstairs, Em. If you need anything, please just come up and knock. Okay?"

"I will." Liam felt her squeeze his hand slightly, and he squeezed back in return. "Thank you again for this morning. And for fixing the window. And lunch. It was delicious. I really appreciate it."

"It's not a problem." Liam waited for a heartbeat. Needing to soak in the sight of her as much as possible before leaving.

Reluctantly, he let go of her hand and instantly missed the warmth. "I'll see you tomorrow."

"Enjoy the rest of your day, Liam."

"You too, Emily." Once again, he stayed planted outside her door until the sound of the lock engaged.

Seven

Liam had come by Emily's flat right at eleven o'clock. She was impressed with his punctuality. The few men she had been on dates with in the past had always been late. Emily had to admit that his ability to be on time impressed her. A lot.

Lexi was ecstatic when Emily had called to tell her about Liam asking her out on a date. It took some time to calm her friend down. In typical Lexi style, she immediately asked Emily for more details about Liam, wanting to know every detail about his looks, to what kind of car he drove. It was only after Emily promised her a full report later that Lexi calmed down and let Emily get to bed.

Although she was excited about the day, the butterflies in her stomach fluttered erratically. She'd gotten ready, choosing to keep her outfit simple and comfortable, slipping on her favorite pair of skinny jeans that molded to her body perfectly. She decided on a lightweight cream color blouse that boasted a "V" neck neckline, and she chose to dress it up with a long necklace. She thought it accented her cleavage just enough, allowing her to feel sexy and confident. She finished the outfit with her favorite open front cardigan. It was just enough to keep her warm in the chilly San Francisco air.

When Liam knocked on the door, Emily's knees almost buckled at the sight of him. He wore dark denim and a white-button up shirt that stretched around his biceps, pulling across his chest. The darkness of his hair contrasted with his crystal blue eyes, reminding her of the aqua hue the moon took on when shining down upon the ocean at night.

He surprised Emily by saying they were going to ride the Cable Car. Emily had never been on a Cable Car and was impressed with the whole experience. Riding in the open-air streetcar was exhilarating. She had never ridden public transportation that allowed the wind to blow through her hair and brush her face. She hadn't expected the experience to be as enjoyable as it was. When the Cable Car came to the top of the steep hills before descending, Liam put his arm around her shoulders and whispered assuring words to her, calming her nervousness.

They walked along Pier 39, where they ate lunch at a touristy spot that served Clam Chowder in a Sour Dough bread bowl. The meal was delicious. They walked to Ghirardelli Square, where they indulged in some delightful treats from the famous confectioner shop. Then hopped on the MUNI train back to Pier 39, where they watched the Sea Lions for a while. Liam stood behind Emily on the dock, his arms wrapped around her waist. He pointed out the numerous cities that could be seen around the Bay from their vantage point.

The sun had broken through the clouds by then, warming the air. The slight breeze kept them comfortable but wasn't overpowering. And it was an immaculately clear day. The view of the Golden Gate Bridge sitting at the entrance of the bay was breathtaking. The clear blue sky against the bridge's reddish-orange and the rolling green hills anchoring each end was a sight to behold. If Emily hadn't known any better, she would have thought she was staring at a painting.

When they arrived back at the house later that afternoon, Emily felt amazing. Aside from hanging out with Lexi, she couldn't remember the last time she had so much fun just talking and being with someone. She also couldn't remember ever feeling the sensations she felt when she was around Liam. Especially when they touched.

The first time she shook his hand Emily was sure she had imagined the tingling that traveled from his palm and up her arm. Now that she had spent the day with Liam and felt the sensation every time they touched, she was sure it wasn't her imagination playing tricks on her, and she found herself craving the effect of his skin touching hers.

When Liam walked her to her door, she wanted nothing more than to reach out and pull him close. The feeling shocked her. She had never been around anyone who made her want the affection as badly as she wanted it at that moment.

Emily thought she caught a look of hesitation on Liam's face. He reached his hand out and brushed her cheek. The caress was a gentle graze that left her with a warm shiver, and at that moment, she was sure the fire, which had now been ignited deep within her belly, was set to explode into a roaring flame.

"I had fun today, Em," Liam told her. His voice was deep. Deeper than she had heard it before. A raspy tone, thick with desire. His eyes were heavy, intoxicated.

"So did I."

Liam leaned forward, his eyes focused on hers. They were calm, like a gentle sea lulling her to sleep. She was hypnotized by them. In an instant, Emily was thrown into a dream. One of herself in this very same position against the wall. The hazy image of a man stood in front of her, leaning in just as Liam was. She noticed the surrounding woodwork in the vision was the same as the woodwork in the house she now lived in. Was it the same place? How was that possible? Was the foggy image of the man in front of her Liam or someone else?

Frightened by the sudden onslaught of emotions and confusion, Emily flinched, and the images she saw instantly disappeared, and she could see Liam clearly again, standing in front of her.

"You saw something?" Liam asked. His breathing increased as if he, too, had been startled.

"I—" Emily wasn't sure how to put into words what she had just seen.

"I had a vision," he stated after clearing his throat. "Of you and me, right here in this spot. You saw it, too, didn't you?"

"I'm really confused." Her mind screamed to pull away and run. But her heart refused to allow it. "I don't know what's happening."

"Do you trust me?"

Emily swallowed hard and inhaled deeply, trying to slow her heart rate. "I probably shouldn't, but I do."

Liam's hand moved from her cheek to the back of her neck, where he gently caressed her skin, sending more electrical pulses down her spine.

"We will figure out what is going on. Something is happening. I don't know what it is just yet, but I'm going to find out. That being said, there is something about you. I feel this connection to you that I've never felt before. I can't stop thinking about you. I don't know what happened a minute ago, but I hope it doesn't frighten you to the point where you pull away from me. There's a link between us, and I'd like to explore that if you're open to it."

Emily stared into Liam's ultramarine eyes, and what she saw was a gentleness she had never seen in anyone before. After what just happened, she should feel terrified. Instead, the need to be near him overtook her senses. "I'm not afraid," she said. Her hands had found their way to his arms, and she held on to him, relishing in the feeling of him caging her between himself and the wall behind her. "I don't know what this is either, but I'm comfortable with you. I've never felt that before. I feel like I've known you forever. I should be terrified right now by what I just saw, but I'm not."

Liam nodded and smiled. "I'm beyond relieved to hear that."

He continued to lean forward, and for a moment, Emily thought he was going to kiss her. Only he angled his head at the last second and placed his lips on her cheek. The moment his lips touched her skin, the energy between them increased. The voided space between their bodies pulsed and Emily thought the lights in the chandelier hanging above them flickered.

"Did you see that?" Emily asked, needing confirmation that she hadn't imagined the phenomenon.

"I did," Liam answered, not moving his gaze from her.

She inhaled his spicy, musky scent, sending shock waves through her. "Liam?"

His gaze met hers, eyes crystal blue and intense as if they were begging for an answer to his already unasked question. "Yes, Em?" his voice was a half-whisper.

"Would you like to stay for dinner?"

Liam pressed himself against her slightly. She wasn't scared of him. In fact, she welcomed the heat of his body.

Liam leaned down, looking directly into her eyes. "You want me to stay for dinner?"

"Y-yes. I'm asking you if you would like to stay for dinner. It's nothing fancy. But if you—"

"Emily," he said, placing his finger on her lips to stop her.

She stared up at him, their bodies now so close her chest was touching his. Vibrations of electrical currents flew between them, and her breath escaped her in short waves that made her head spin with lust.

"I would love to stay for dinner."

"Oh. Okay. Good," Emily said on a long breath.

"What are we having?"

"I was going to roast some chicken."

"Good," Liam shifted his hand and touched his knuckles to her cheek, tracing her jawline and tucking some of her hair behind her ear. "I love roasted chicken."

Not sure why, perhaps it was the closeness, but deep down, she knew it was because it was Liam. Emily's heart rate quickened, and her cheeks burned. Her stomach fluttered, and girly parts tingled. She hated to admit it, but Lexi had been right. She was going to fall hard and fast for this man. And if she was being completely honest with herself, that's exactly what she wanted.

"Do you need any help with cooking?"

"Uh, no. It won't take me long to prep it."

"Okay, do you mind if I run upstairs real quick?" He took a step back, stealing the delicious sensation coursing through her body. She instantly missed the warmth radiating off of him.

"No, of course not. I'll leave the door unlocked for you," she told him.

"Okay. I'll be back."

She nodded at him, and he turned to head upstairs. She stepped into her flat, kicked off her shoes, hung her sweater and purse on the hook near the door, and grabbed her phone. Emily hurried to the kitchen to start dinner. But first things first, she swiped open the text app and began typing. Lexi was going to die when she heard how her date went.

***

The shadow lurked at the end of the hallway, seething as Liam touched *his* treasured gem. It watched as *his* darling gazed into another's eye, becoming lost in a lust he wished was for him. She was supposed to be his. He should have been the axis on which her world revolved upon. Not the other man's. What was it about his rival that had his beloved seduced? His plans had been perfect. Everything had been set. He could have given her everything she desired, yet she still gravitated towards the one man he despised.

Memories of his demise floated forth, tormenting him, of how he left the physical world before fully being able to enjoy the riches he had collected. Reminding him of the deeds he'd done.

Eight

Of course he wanted to stay. The thought of leaving her tonight was killing him. She caught him off guard. He assumed maybe she'd need some space and time to think about the vision they had both shared. Liam couldn't decide if he would bring up what he had discussed with his friends the previous day. He knew he should, especially after their linked visions. Knew she deserved to know why he felt so connected to her. But, the thought of laying all of that information on her weighed on him.

Liam pulled his phone from his back pocket and typed.

Liam: She asked me over for dinner.

Trey: No shit! You said yes, right?

Liam: Yeah. I said yes.

Luke: You're one lucky SOB.

Trey: I've been thinking about our past cases. Remember the Walters case from 2006?

Luke: Oh shit! I forgot about that!

Liam: Yeah. I remember. I know where you're going and to tell you the truth, I don't even want to think about it right now.

Liam rubbed his hands across his face. The Walters case had been one of the toughest cases they had investigated to date. The couple had been tormented by an entity for decades. It wasn't until Liam and his team stepped in when they uncovered the truth about a gruesome murder that was linked to the Walters from decades earlier.

Luke: Alright. Let us know how dinner goes.
Liam: I will

Liam headed back downstairs. Emily had done what she said and left her front door unlocked for him. At first, the idea of her leaving her door unlocked made him nervous, but with the front door to the building always being locked and him being the only other resident in the house, he figured there wasn't too much to worry about.

Knocking as he opened the door, he peeked his head in and entered. Emily was standing in the kitchen, seasoning some chicken leg quarters and placing them on a baking pan. There was a loaf of bread sitting on the counter and a bowl of chopped potatoes and onions.

She looked gorgeous standing there. She had put her hair in a loose bun on top of her head, and golden curls framed her face. She sniffled and blinked rapidly, allowing a tear to escape the corner of her eye. He strode to her, placing his finger under her chin, forcing her to look up at him. "What's wrong?" he asked.

"What?" Confusion swept across her face. Blinking again, more tears fell down her cheek. "Oh! I'm okay. I was slicing those onions. Onions always make me cry like this."

Liam let out a breath and stepped back. His gut still wrenched from seeing the kaleidoscopes play in her eyes, he watched as Emily continued to prepare dinner. "I've never seen roasted chicken prepared that way," he said as Emily spread the chopped onions and potatoes next to the chicken on the pan before placing everything in the waiting hot oven. Then she went to wash her hands.

Laughing, she answered, "Well. It's normally just me. This is a lot easier than roasting a whole chicken. And it's just as good.'

A buzzing sounded on the opposite counter. "Oh, that's just my best friend, Lexi. I told her you were staying for dinner and she's worried."

Liam grinned. "It sounds like she's looking out for you."

Emily scrunched her nose while staring at her phone, and her brows drew together.

"What is it?"

"Oh. She's paranoid. I love her to death, though. She's worried that I'm alone with you in my apartment. So, I told her I would call her a little later to check in."

"Give her a call now." Liam casually leaned against the counter opposite of her, resting his hands behind him.

"What?" Emily asked.

"Call her. Tell her I'm happy to answer any of her questions."

Emily raised her eyebrows. "Okay, but I'm warning you now, she's a firecracker." Emily pressed the call button on her phone and briefly spoke to her friend before holding her hand out to Liam. "Here you go," she said with a sexy smirk.

He took the phone. "Hello, this is Liam Wesley," he said as he gave Emily a wink. "I know Emily is your best friend. She's very lucky to have you. I can assure you that you have nothing to worry about." Pause. "No, I haven't dated in quite a while."

"Oh my God! Alexis. Knock it off!" Emily shouted.

Liam took her hand and led her into the living room, where they both sat down on her sofa. Liam placed both of their hands on his knee. He hadn't meant for the affectionate gesture to happen, and for a second considered letting go. But when he felt Emily relax and give his hand a slight squeeze, he decided to leave them where they were and continued with Lexi. "I completely understand. I would never do anything to hurt Em." Pause. "I have every intention of taking her on a dinner date. In fact, I was planning on asking her out tomorrow night for dinner, but she beat me to it." Pause. "Oh yeah, she's blushing real hard. She's as red as a beef-steak tomato."

Emily jumped up and tried to grab the phone from Liam, but he pulled her back down, this time onto his lap. He laughed and said his goodbye to Lexi before hanging up.

"What the fuck did she say?"

"Easy, Em." He couldn't control his laughter. She was right. Lexi was definitely a firecracker. "Lexi just had some advice for me. Mostly along the lines of if I dared hurt you in any way, she'd be on the first plane down here and rip my throat out. She also knew you've been wanting to get to know me better, and she's glad you worked up the nerve to ask me over for dinner. When she asked if I was planning on taking you out to dinner, she knew you were blushing and asked for confirmation. I can't lie to your best friend, babe."

The feeling of Emily in his lap was both soothing and unbearable. He wrapped his arm around her, holding her. Her legs draped over the side of his, and he savored the feel of her.

Emily sighed heavily. "She can be so nosy."

"She's a good friend and is looking out for you."

"That was embarrassing."

Liam pulled Emily closer. Their faces were almost close enough for him to place a kiss on her lips. Her sweet scent combined with the sight of her rosy lips made his mouth water. Liam reached a hand up and cupped the back of her head while his other arm held her firmly around her waist. "That was adorable." Liam tugged her head toward him slightly, and Emily responded willingly, lowering her head farther. Their lips met in a soft brush. A delicate kiss that sparked a current of pleasure through Liam's body. His hand found its way under her shirt, where he touched the bare skin of her back.

Emily pulled back, her eyes closed. The beautiful smile and dusty pink hue across her chest faded, and she drew in a shaky breath. She opened her eyes and glanced down the hallway. Liam felt small tremors under his fingers that were at her back. She was shaking and had gone pale.

"Liam," she said hesitantly.

"What is it?" Emily's eyes stayed fixated down the hall. Liam followed her gaze.

What he saw was enough to cause the blood to leave his own face too. The feeling in the room grew heavy with oppression. The air was ice cold. Like a blanket of dread had come down on them.

Standing halfway in the bedroom doorway and halfway in the hallway was a large shadow figure of a man. Devoid of any features, standing there. Watching them.

Not breaking eye contact with the apparition, he tightened his hold around Emily and whispered, "Em, grab your phone and pull up the camera. Now."

With extremely shaky hands, she reached down and picked up her phone sitting next to him. "You have a better angle than I do. Take pictures of it."

She did. She probably took a hundred pictures. Liam could hear the shutter click continuously. Fuck, she was smart. He knew she held her thumb on the shutter button in an attempt to catch the figure on one of the photos.

Then, it was gone, vanishing before their eyes as it took a step back into the bedroom. The air was still frigidly cold and felt charged, like when a lightning storm is passing through. Liam turned to Emily. "Did you get a good shot?"

"I think so." Hands still shaking, she flipped through the images. "Here. Here it is."

Half of a black, featureless figure stood in the doorway down the hall on the screen.

"Will you send that one to me? I'm going to send it to my team."

Without answering, Emily did as he asked. In seconds, his phone chimed at the successful delivery of the text message containing the image. He helped Emily scoot on to the sofa. When he stood up, he bent over her, hugging her head and whispered in her ear, "You wait here, okay? I'm going to go take a look."

She nodded her head, and before walking to the hallway, he sent his friends a message with the image:

Liam: Get to my place, now! Bring equipment.

While he slowly made his way down the hall, he heard his phone chime twice. His friends were on their way.

Nine

Other than a lingering chill and slight prickling sensation, causing the hairs on Liam's arms to stand on end, there was no sign of the shadow he and Emily had just seen. He thought about doing an EVP session, where he would attempt to capture disembodied voices on a recording device, only he didn't have his recorder on him. There had never been a reason for him to carry it when he wasn't investigating. Though now, he thought maybe it would be a good idea to keep it on him.

When he stepped into the kitchen, a bottle of wine sitting on the counter caught his eye. Emily must have planned on opening it for dinner as she had set up the wine key and two wine glasses next to it. Liam walked over and removed the foil from around the opening. He inserted the worm of the corkscrew, twisting it until it was fully inserted. He folded the lever end down over the bottle and used the leverage to pull the cork free. Then, he poured a generous amount into the glasses.

Carrying a glass in each hand, Liam found Emily still sitting on the sofa where he had left her in the living room. With fingers frantically moving across the screen of her phone, Liam assumed she was texting Lexi to let her know what had just happened. "Em?

I'm having my team head over here right now."

Not looking up at him, her knuckles white from gripping the phone so tightly. She acknowledged his statement by saying, "Okay."

Liam placed the glasses down on the coffee table and sat down next to her. "Are you texting Lexi?"

"Yes. She's freaking out because I'm freaking out. Now, I'm trying to calm her down."

"Why don't you call her? She'll feel better if she hears your voice."

Emily nodded in agreement before sending off one last text message. Three seconds later, her phone rang. Emily sat and talked to Lexi, doing her best to reassure her she was okay. A minute later, Emily held the phone out to Liam. "She wants to talk to you."

Liam took the phone. "Hello, Lexi?"

"Is Em really okay? She doesn't sound okay."

"She is physically just fine. Emotionally, right now, she's shaken up, as am I."

"Don't leave her alone," Lexi stated. Liam stole a glance in Emily's direction. She rested her head against the back of the sofa. Her eyes were closed as she breathed deeply. "She will kill me for telling you this, but she has anxiety. She's in a new place that is haunted. I'm not there to help comfort her. I don't want her to have a panic attack while alone."

Listening to Lexi's concern for her friend was sweet. It reminded Liam of his friendship with Trey and Luke. They looked out for one another.

"You don't have to worry about that, Lexi. I wasn't going to."

He heard Lexi breathe a sharp sigh of relief. "Okay. Good. I can't believe this is happening to her. She's never had to deal with anything on this level before."

"What do you mean?" Liam calmly interrupted and lowered his voice.

Lexi was silent for a moment. Liam heard a sharp intake of breath on the other end. "I'll let her tell you."

Liam kept his gaze on Emily. Had she been dealing with a haunting prior to moving to San Francisco? He had seen what stress of hauntings could do to a person. Victims normally tried to go about their lives and ignore the activity taking place around them, until it became too much. Most people only called in help once they had reached their breaking point. There was no way he was letting that happen to Emily. "We are going to find out what is going on. She won't be here alone until we get rid of this thing. My friends and teammates are on their way over right now."

"Alright. I know you like Em. And she's going to kill me for saying this too, but I think it needs to be said. She likes you. A lot." Liam's heart jumped into his throat at Lexi's statement. Knowing that Emily had spoken to her best friend about him and confessed her attraction to him made his own knees weak. "She's had bad luck with guys. Don't add yourself to that list, okay?"

"I understand, Lexi. I'm on the same page, believe me. My team will be here shortly. I need to talk to them. Don't worry about Em. I'll take care of her. And I will make sure she calls you first thing in the morning."

At that, he and Lexi said their goodbyes, and he hung up. He set Emily's phone down. She had drawn her legs up, hugging them to her chest and head buried in her knees.

He sat on the wooden coffee table, positioned himself in front of her, leaned in, and pulled her close. Emily dropped her feet so they rested on the floor and wrapped her arms around his waist. Her head rested on his shoulder. Liam hugged her tightly, and fuck if his heart didn't skip a beat at the sensation of her body pressed against his. "I poured us both some wine."

"Thank you," Emily said as she lifted her head.

"Here you go." Liam let her go and handed a glass to her. "It will take my friends a little while to get here." He held his own glass in his hand and stared at Emily as she took a sip of the golden liquid. "Will you tell me the passcode to your phone?"

Emily stared at him in confusion.

"Lexi is someone who you care about. And she cares about you. I want to make sure I can contact her in case you can't for any reason."

"That's sweet of you," Emily told him and gave him the six-digit code to access her phone. She took another sip of wine and smiled at him over the rim of her glass. "Tell me, how did you get into paranormal investigating?"

Looking at his glass, Liam took a breath. "Well, now that's an interesting story."

"Good. I like interesting stories," she said as she tipped her glass to her lips, taking another delicate taste of the wine.

Smiling at her, Liam took one of her hands in his. He wanted to feel her warmth while he explained the reasons behind his infatuation with Parapsychology. "It started when I was a kid. We moved into this house up in Sacramento. From the outside, it looked like any of the other houses on the block. But the place was so haunted. There was ghostly activity almost daily. We all started having experiences from the start."

"Wow. What kind of things happened? If you don't mind me asking?"

"No, not at all. It all started out pretty mild. We would notice that things would be moved around the house from where we set them down. A light would be on when we knew we turned it off. We would find doors open when we knew we shut them. But it started to escalate quickly. We all began having nightmares. We would be touched by something that we couldn't see. Noises, like footsteps, were heard in rooms we knew were empty. The final straw was when we came home after my dad had picked my brothers, sister, and I up from school one afternoon. We found my mom at the bottom of the stairs. She said something had pushed her down."

"Oh my god! Was she hurt?" Emily squeezed his hand, then stroked it with her thumb.

"She was okay, thankfully. She had a hurt ankle, but nothing too serious. My dad called in everyone he could think of at the time to help us. A priest, even a Rabbi, and a Native American Shaman. Anyone he could get to listen and who was willing to come out to the house. There weren't many people doing paranormal investigations in those days, and the internet wasn't what it is today. Research and finding people to help was harder. Eventually, we moved, and the activity stopped for us."

"Wow," Emily said. The look on her face was worrisome.

Afraid he was frightening her, he chose to wrap up his response. "So, that's how it all started for me. I wanted to help people who were experiencing what I did. First, to let people know that they are not crazy. Unexplainable things do happen, and just because we can't find an explanation for certain circumstances doesn't mean that they aren't real. They shouldn't be ignored, especially when it affects a person's life. Second, to try and find out the truth. What really does happen when someone passes on? Why do some people choose to stay behind, and some supposedly move on? There are so many questions in this world. Way more questions than answers. I want to try and find some of those answers."

"That's wonderful. You're passionate about your work. That's so admirable. How many siblings do you have?"

"I have two brothers and a baby sister."

Emily smiled. "You have a big family."

Liam chuckled and nodded, looking into her eyes. "I do. I have a bunch of nieces and nephews too. Holidays are always fun." Liam caught a hint of sadness in Emily at his last statement. "How about you, Em? Tell me about you."

"Well…" she began and held her wine glass to her lips again. "There isn't much to talk about. I didn't have a family when I was young. I grew up in foster care."

Liam stopped mid-sip and lowered his glass back down. "Wow. I'm sorry."

"It's okay."

"When did you go into foster care?" he asked.

"My entire life. My mother surrendered me at a fire station. I was told that I was only a few hours old. Social services assumed my mother was a drug addict and possibly homeless. There were drugs found in my system at the hospital. After I went through withdrawals, I was placed in foster care. I wasn't one of the lucky ones to be adopted. I was completely on my own when I graduated high school. And I've been completely on my own since."

Fucking Hell, he thought. It was one thing to be abandoned at birth, but it was a whole other thing to have to spend your entire childhood in foster care.

"Wow. I'm sorry, Em. Really."

Emily lifted one shoulder in a shrug and brought her legs back up to sit cross-legged. She played with the rim of her glass while she spoke. "It's okay. I've made peace with it. I was angry for a long time. But, I decided I didn't want to be angry at people who I didn't even know anymore. In college, I majored in art with an emphasis in photography. It always made me happy. I got through school and established my career."

Since she was at a point where she felt comfortable opening up to him, Liam asked, "Did you ever live in a foster home where there was any paranormal activity?"

Emily hesitated to answer.

"I'm asking only because I'm trying to figure out what is going on here. Hauntings don't normally just start out of the blue without something significant happening. I'm not saying you have anything to do with what's going on here. I'm just trying to put pieces together."

"Liam," she said. She looked directly into his eyes, conflict stirring in them.

"It's okay. I won't judge you. What is it?"

"I've experienced a haunting my entire life."

Liam froze. "What?"

"I know it sounds strange, but it's true. Though it's never been this severe. It's actually worsened since moving here. I never thought what I experienced would ever affect anyone else. I'm so sorry if I brought something h—,"

He cut her off, "Stop. Don't you dare apologize." Looking at her, Liam softened his stare and placed her wine glass on the table beside his own. He took her other hand. "This is not your fault, and it's also not strange. Millions of people experience some kind of haunting every year. You are not alone in this."

"If I had known, I would have never come here."

"Don't say that. I'm glad you're here," Liam said in a half-whisper while leaning in closer to her.

"What?" Emily gasped, surprised.

"I said I'm glad you are here," he reiterated and reached up to tuck a lock of her hair behind her ear, making sure he allowed the palm of his hand to brush her cheek in the process. "Tell me what you've experienced throughout your life. It might be helpful for me and the team to know."

Emily closed her eyes and took a cleansing breath. "I've always dealt with sleep paralysis. I didn't know what it was until I was in high school, though."

"Sleep paralysis," he confirmed. "It's when the brain is not fully awake and keeps your body in the REM state. You're conscious, but you're also paralyzed," he explained, trying to comfort her by letting her know he understood what the condition was. "It can be terrifying, from what I've read."

Emily nodded. "It is. It was a relief to finally know that I wasn't crazy when I learned what it is. But the only time I experience it is after I have a reoccurring dream. A dream I've had for as long as I can remember."

Liam's heart felt like it was going to beat right out of his chest. Was she experiencing the same dream he was? Did she recognize him too? Was she aware of their relationship in the dream? "What is the dream about?"

She took another deep breath and said, "I'm in a dark place. I can hear voices, but I can't make out what they are saying. And I can't make out the figures. It's all blurry. But I know I'm lying down, and I'm hurt and can't move. And then I wake up. Only when I wake, I can't move, and I always feel a presence near me."

Liam's heart raced. She confirmed that she couldn't clearly see the people in her dream. So there was no way of knowing if she shared the same nightmare. "What kind of presence?"

"A terrible one," she confirmed. Tears escaped the corners of her eyes. "I've only told two other people about this. One is Lexi. And the other was an old boyfriend I had a few years ago. He was a phycologist, and he thought I was delusional and wanted me to take medication."

"Fucking dick." Liam couldn't believe how insensitive some people could be. Emily's lips curled into a smile, bringing him a little comfort that he was able to lighten the mood with his comment. "What about this presence is terrible?"

"I don't know. It's an oppressive feeling, I guess. Like, it's angry and wants me to be scared. It's so hard to explain. When I see the shadow figure—,"

Cutting her off quickly. "Wait! You've seen the shadow figure before moving here?"

"Yes," Emily confirmed. "Only never like what we just saw. It's never come at me like it did in the bathroom. I've always seen it out of the corner of my eye or at a distance, and it was always gone in the blink of an eye. It's never hung around like it did."

Holy Shit! He was not expecting this.

"I think it's the reason why I was never adopted. My foster families never said anything directly to me, but I've always felt that whatever this thing is, doesn't want me to have a family. Doesn't want me to be with anyone or be happy."

"What makes you think that?"

"Because every time I have the opportunity to date, the activity around me picks up. The presence follows me wherever I go, and the dreams happen more frequently. They make me stressed and exhausted. And when I move on from the idea of dating, everything around me subsides. As a kid, whenever I was placed with a family and things went great, and I would think maybe this would be the family to adopt me, activity in the house would start, and I would be moved and placed with another family."

"Have you had these dreams and sleep paralysis since you arrived in San Francisco?"

"Yes." She squeezed his hand, hard. "At first, maybe just once a week. Lately, it's been more frequent, every night." Emily stared at her hands resting in his. Liam used his thumbs to caress her skin.

The knowledge that the presence around Emily had tormented her for years pissed Liam off. And the fact that it had grown more severe simply because she was talking to him made his blood boil. But he pushed that anger aside to focus entirely on the woman sitting in front of him, a woman who he knew his entire life in a dream. But now, she sat in flesh and bone, holding his hand. "Emily, we will figure this all out. I need you to believe that. Okay?"

"Okay." She sniffed, giving Liam a small nod.

Noticing the room was chilled, Liam took the blanket that was draped over the back of the sofa and wrapped it around Emily. For the first time in his life, he thought, what the fuck was up with ghosts and the cold? He had been ghost hunting for years. Had felt hundreds of cold spots, but had never given any thought as to why apparitions choose to suck the life from a room.

His rational mind told him it was simply the need for energy that they were seeking to manifest some sort of phenomenon. But his protective heart was pissed off at the idea that the occurrence was making the woman he cared about uncomfortable.

Knocking at the front door to the building pulled Liam from his thoughts. "I have to go let Trey and Luke in. We are going to come right back in here. I'll leave your front door open. Stay right here."

Not wanting to leave her, but knowing it was necessary, Liam picked up her glass of wine from the table and placed it in her hands, hoping that would help her mind focus on something other than what was happening around her. He walked to the front of the house, cursing himself at the thought that his two best friends didn't have a key to his building. Making a mental note to correct that soon, he met Trey and Luke at the front door and let them in.

They both held a couple of cameras, and each had a large duffel bag that carried extra batteries, cables, and laptop computers. "Thanks, guys," he told them.

Both men greeted Liam and stepped through the threshold of the Victorian home. Trey and Luke were both big men. Taller than Liam and more muscular. Luke had a rugged look, light hair and skin, and a beard that he kept slightly longer than Liam's closely shaved look. He also had a bad boy persona—intimidating looking at times. He was an unyielding warrior who stood his ground but had the biggest heart and his intentions were always for helping and making sure the well-being of their clients was number one priority. "Don't even mention it. Where is she?" Trey asked.

Liam gestured a few feet away at the open door, and Trey proceeded into the flat where Emily was waiting.

"I have recorders with me and the EMF meter too. Go talk to Trey while I walk through the house and see if I get any strange readings. Is it okay if I go into the basement?"

That was Luke. Always ready and willing to investigate at a moment's notice. Liam had never met anyone as enthusiastic about provoking and urging an entity to show itself as Luke was. Liam hadn't known Luke as long as he knew Trey, but Luke was his other right-hand man nonetheless.

Putting his hand on Luke's shoulder, he gave his friend a squeeze, and looking him dead in the eye, he said, "Thank you."

Luke responded, "Not a problem. I got this," and took off down the hallway to get to work.

Back in Emily's living room, Trey had already introduced himself and was making small talk with her as he unpacked his duffel bag. Trey, also being a big man, took up much of the small space in the corner of the living room. He was the epitome of tall, dark, and handsome, with a chestnut skin tone and deep brown eyes.

Liam felt relief as it looked like the color was finally returning to her cheeks, and she smiled while engaging in small talk with Trey.

"Stay away from her, Trey. She's mine," Liam told his friend, playfully. Trey dropped his head down and grinned.

Emily blushed as she curled her lips up, giving him a sexy smile that caused his heart to flutter. "What did Lexi say to you?"

"Nothing I wasn't already planning on doing."

Liam took a seat next to Emily, putting his hand in hers. They both described what had happened as Trey readied his recorder and a couple of cameras.

"Okay. I know Luke is getting some readings around the house. Since there has already been activity, I expect there to be some strange readings. But we'll see if he catches anything really out of the norm. Have you been back in the bedroom?"

"Yeah. After Em took the pictures, I walked down the hall and took a look around in there. It was cold as fuck and staticky. Really charged up. All the hairs on my arms stood on end. But that's it."

"Alright. Let me go to the bedroom with a recorder and a camera. I'll see if I can catch anything. I'm not going to provoke. Not yet. You guys are sleeping in this building, and I don't want to make the situation worse for you two. Have you heard back from Phil?"

"No. I haven't. And I'm getting worried."

"We'll deal with that later. You two stay here. I want to see if this thing will show itself to me."

Liam nodded as Trey stood and made his way down the hallway, voice recorder, and camera in hand.

Ten

Luke wished he had grabbed a walkie talkie before leaving his house, but in a rush to get to Liam, the thought slipped his mind. Making a mental note not to let that happen again, he continued down the steps to the basement.

He didn't detect any abnormal readings in Liam's flat, but he couldn't ignore the sick, anxious feeling in the pit of his stomach. It was the same sense he got every time they investigated an active location. A combination of excitement and dread flooded his gut, causing his adrenaline to spike and his stomach to roll. He knew there was something there, and the fact that he had never felt anything like it before when he came to the house to visit Liam, pissed him off. What kind of dormant fucked up shit was hiding this whole time and no one knew about it? And why was it messing with his friend's girl? That was the most confusing part about the situation. What was the connection between Liam and Emily?

At the bottom of the stairs, Luke rounded the corner and began asking questions in hopes that the recorder would pick up a disembodied voice. Checking the EMF detector and seeing that the baseline hadn't changed, he turned left toward the furnace. Liam said he'd seen the shadow figure there the night that the pilot light in Emily's furnace went out, so it seemed like a good place to do a recording session. Luke noticed a door with a padlock on it as he stepped on to the concrete slab of the lower level foundation. He had never been in the basement before and wasn't aware of an apartment down there. Seeing the padlock on the door, he wondered why old Phil would keep it locked. *Storage maybe?*

As he passed the door, the EMF detector spiked. Double checking that the recording device was on, he spoke, making sure to wait a few seconds between each question.

"What's your name?"

Silence.

"Where are you from?"

Silence.

"Why are you here?"

Silence.

"What do you want?"

The EMF detector spiked again, lighting up all of the indicators and sounding a buzzer. The hairs on Luke's neck stood straight up. "I know you're here. I can feel you. Speak into this thing I'm holding and tell me your name," Luke stated as he held the voice recorder in the air.

The lights on the EMF meter continued to light up erratically while he stood in front of the locked door. There was something behind it that disrupted the electromagnetic field. Wanting to see if there were any other unusual readings in the basement, Luke walked away and swept the rest of the area, stopping at the furnace to ask another round of questions. Noting that the EMF detector wasn't picking up any readings, he walked back toward the apartment door and picked up high fluctuations again. Pulling his cell phone from his pocket, Luke sent Liam a quick text.

Luke: In the basement. Getting readings by apartment door. Will check recorder when done.

Two seconds later, Liam's response came through.
Liam: Copy that. Reconvene up here in 10.
Luke: Copy that

***

Trey was in Emily's bedroom about to wrap up an EVP session. He'd closed the door to prevent any contaminating noise from entering the room since Emily and Liam were still in the living room.

Trey sat on the end of her lofty bed with an infrared camera, and he placed a voice recorder on the dresser across from the bed. He had done a quick review after each round of questions, but hadn't captured any disembodied voices.

The room was an icebox. Despite the warm, charming decor and plush bedding and pillows, an uncomfortable presence was near. Trey could hear the hum of the furnace through the vents. He walked over to the far wall and placed his hand in front of the heat register. Warm air blew against his skin. It was evident that whatever was present was having a significant effect on the environment.

The static in the air that Liam had mentioned was still palpable. Like the feeling from back in the days when someone had left one of those boxy, old fashioned TV's on in a room. You knew the TV was on by the way all of your hairs would stand up, and your ears would ring, your body felt engulfed by an invisible energy. That was the feeling of Emily's bedroom. Only there was no TV present.

Trey had already taken dozens of photos with a small digital camera, but nothing had shown up. He was eager to do a full investigation of the place. He wished he'd grabbed more equipment, but there wasn't enough time. Liam had sent the photo of a shadow figure standing in the doorway, and he asked for help. Since Luke and Trey were roommates, they made quick work of gathering what they deemed most essential, but had missed packing the motion sensors and other investigation equipment that could be useful.

Trey kept the work van parked at his house since he had the room, but he never stored their expensive gear inside of it. What they had on them wasn't ideal, but it would do for a spur of the moment investigation where activity had been witnessed recently.

Trey walked back out to the hallway and decided to snap pictures throughout the rest of the flat. Just as he was about to say something to Liam and Emily, Luke walked through the front door, eyes wide. Trey knew that look.

Before Trey or Liam could say anything, Luke said, "Guys, we need to talk."

Liam stood from the sofa. "What did you find?"

"I caught some EVPs. I can make out a couple on the recorder, but there's one that needs to be cleaned up. Should I go to the van to work on it?"

Trey watched as Liam turned to Emily. He knew his friend was debating whether he should let her listen to the EVPs now or wait. Before Liam could ask the question, Emily spoke up, "I would like to hear them. If it's okay with you."

Liam didn't move his gaze from Emily. He stared at her with warm affection, her eyes meeting his with the same emotion. "Luke, go get whatever you need from the van and set up here. We'll all listen to it together."

Luke glanced over, and Trey gave a subtle nod before his friend turned to walk out to the van. Trey picked up his laptop bag and set himself up at the small dining table where he wrote up a report on the residence.

Eleven

Emily walked up to Liam after taking the food out of the oven and placing it in containers. The guys had stopped to review the voice recorders, double-checking that they hadn't missed any voices being picked up, and Luke was working on cleaning up an EVP that he'd caught. Her appetite had disappeared, and Liam had said he was no longer hungry. She figured it would be nice to have leftovers at the ready, and maybe she and Liam could enjoy the food another night. After she placed the containers in the refrigerator, she made her way into the living room.

Emily listened to the three friends discuss the night's events using paranormal jargon. She was feeling a little excluded. Not because she felt ignored, but because she wasn't understanding a lot of the terminology being used. Sure, she had watched some ghost hunting shows on TV, but it was a whole other experience being in the presence of paranormal investigators and watching them work. Seeing Liam in his element, working and talking about types of EVPs so passionately, turned her on even more.

Emily had made up her mind during their brief kiss on the sofa that she wasn't letting the spirit skew her feelings or desires any longer. She didn't care if her thoughts spurred more activity around her. Perhaps that would help Liam discover who the entity was, and they could get rid of it. Emily let herself relish in the sight of Liam, in her living room, working and looking like the finest specimen of a man she'd ever seen.

"Okay. I've cleaned this one EVP up as best I can," Luke said from the dining table. The previous two EVPs were not hard to make out. They all listened to them right after Luke set up his computer. Both sounded deep, menacing, and like they came from the same voice. A creepy feeling of familiarity, yet Emily couldn't connect the dots as to why. They spoke, "I'm here," and "She's mine."

Emily slipped her arm around Liam's waist, and he pulled her close, his arm resting over her shoulders. He held her securely to him. She shivered in his embrace. Not from cold and not from discomfort. She simply hadn't yet grown used to the fiery jolt that coursed through her body whenever they touched. As electrifying as it was, she craved the feeling all the same and looked forward to the sensation. "What's an EVP?" she asked.

Luke spoke up, still sitting at the makeshift workstation that was her dinette table. "We're sorry, Emily. We didn't mean to leave you out. An EVP is an Electronic Voice Phenomena. A voice that we can't hear with our own ears in the moment but records itself on a device, and we can replay it back after it's been captured."

"I see."

"Here it is. It sounds grainy, but it's the best I can do. It's said right after, 'She's mine,' and it sounds like it's the same voice." Luke handed a set of noise-canceling headphones to Liam and plugged them into the laptop.

"We use the headphones to block out any background noise so we can listen more closely to the EVP," Liam told her. Looking at Luke, he gave his friend a nod before saying, "Go ahead."

Liam closed his eyes, dropped his head, and listened to the

recording, cupping the earpieces with his hands, as if he were trying to press the sound closer to his eardrums. After a few moments, he removed the headphones and gave them to Trey so he could listen. After another few moments, Trey looked up. "Emily?" he asked, "Do you want to listen?"

"Yes," she answered with certainty and confidence.

Emily took the headphones from Trey. Before she placed them on her ears, Liam told her, "It's a whisper, and it's playing on a loop. You'll hear it play over and over. Let us know what you think it's saying."

"Okay." She placed the headphones over her ears and was thrown into a state of odd deafness. With the lack of ambient noise and the rushing sound of her own blood through her ears, she felt vulnerable. Making eye contact with Luke, she gave him a small nod and said, "I'm ready."

Emily watched as Luke pressed a button, and the sound of faint white noise filled her head. Then, the sound she was waiting to hear came through the headphones, sending an icy chill down her spine. Though it was a whisper, it resonated a deep, gruff, and threatening tone. It played repeatedly, with only a second between each loop. When she couldn't take any more of the ominous voice, she pulled the headphones off.

"I think I hear 'Abigail.'"

"Yeah. That's what we hear too," Liam confirmed.

"Who is Abigail?"

Liam looked at her, shaking his head. "I don't know. Trey, have you been able to find anything out?"

"No, nothing yet. It's like this place was just built and nothing has ever happened here. I can't even come up with any police reports, death records. Nothing."

"Man, have you talked to Phil yet?" Luke asked. "I really want to get into that room in the basement. The EMF detector was going nuts outside the door. And that's where I caught all of the EVPs. I wanna know what's in there."

"No. I was telling Trey, I can't get a hold of him. I'm getting worried too. He always gets back to me. I wanna do another investigation as soon as we can." Liam paused for a moment, rubbing his hand down his face, stopping at his chin, he stroked the light stubble. "We'll get into the apartment and just replace the lock. I agree. We need to know what's in there. I don't think he'll be upset. I'll explain to him that it was imperative. He knows what we do for work. I think he'll understand our reasons for going in."

A flicker caught the corner of Emily's eye. Liam must have noticed it too. His arm tightened around her just as she turned her head toward the floor lamp in the living room. All of the lights were now pulsing and buzzing from the fluctuating electrical currents passing through them.

A crash resounded and the apartment vibrated while a blast of wind rushed through. It traveled low to the floor before ascending where the friends stood at the table, picking up Emily's hair, twirling it around. Liam, Trey, and Luke rushed into the living room. Emily followed behind them, where they found the front window swinging open. It had blown open so hard that the glass had completely shattered.

"What the fuck!" Liam shouted, stalking to the far end of the living room to inspect the window. "I installed these latches myself. There's no way wind or anything natural could do this."

Emily's breath caught at the sight before her. The fact that the windowpane had shattered wasn't what caused her concern. No, what caused the shiver to spread through her and fill her with dread was the pulverized glass that sprinkled her flat, like fine sand. It covered every inch of her floor and furniture in white powdery dust.

The realization set in. This haunting was dangerous. It was growing stronger, and it was hostile. And, it was capable of hurting her.

***

"Emily, don't move! You're not wearing shoes," Liam warned, as he went to the front door where she had a pair of loafers and brought them to her. Emily slipped her feet in while he grabbed a chair from the dinette table. Emily's body quaked. "Sit here, okay." Liam pressed his forehead to hers before settling her in the seat and walked to where Trey and Luke stood in front of the window. All three men were baffled.

Luke spoke in a hushed tone, "What the fuck is going on here?"

"I don't know. But we need to get to the bottom of it soon," Liam said, not caring that agitation blanketed his tone.

"Tomorrow night then," Luke continued. "We need to find out what is here and get rid of it. You and Emily can't live like this."

"What if she'd been standing near the window when it blew apart?" Liam whispered, his voice wobbled with emotion. He shoved his shaking hands in his pockets.

Trey placed his hand on Liam's shoulder. "But she wasn't." Liam lifted his gaze, meeting Trey's stare, and then Luke.

"Right," he agreed. "Tomorrow."

"Tomorrow," Trey repeated. "We'll get the rest of our equipment in the morning and spend the whole night investigating. I know you two are still getting to know each other, but you can't leave her here alone. She's really shaken up."

"I know. And I'm not planning on it."

"Good. We aren't leaving you guys tonight." Trey glanced at Luke, who gave him a nod. "Luke and I will stay here. We'll board up the window and clean up some of this mess. We'll leave some cameras rolling tonight, maybe something will pick up. Take care of Emily. She's scared shitless. Get her calm. And we'll all talk in the morning."

Liam didn't know what to say. He knew his friends would be there for him. He spent all of his adult life chasing ghosts, but the thought of living through a haunting again shook him. Worse, the reality of Emily being put in more danger because the haunting seemed possessive of her frightened him. Liam knew what malicious entities were capable of. He'd seen it with his own eyes while helping others over the years.

Liam didn't talk much about his paranormal experiences as a child, but Trey and Luke were a part of the select few who knew about what his family had gone through. The guys weren't only friends and teammates, they were as close as brothers. Someone Liam cared about was being haunted. Liam was family, that meant Emily was also like family. He knew they would get to the bottom of it.

Luke spoke again, placing his hand on Liam's shoulder. "Go on, Liam. Take care of Emily. We got your back."

Nodding silently, Liam walked toward Emily. She sat in the chair with her hands under her thighs, shivering. Liam picked her phone up off of the coffee table, tucking it in his pocket before kneeling in front of her.

"Emily?" she looked up at him. He knew she was frightened but could see that she was trying to hide it. "You're going to come upstairs to my flat with me." Liam's hand instinctively went to her cheek. Her eyes met his, the browns and golds shimmered in the warm evening light. "Trey and Luke are going to stay in your flat if you're okay with that. They're going to cover the window and leave some cameras rolling through the night."

"O-okay. I'm o-okay with th-that. I'm s-s-orry I c-can't stop s-shaking."

"You have nothing to be sorry for." Liam instinctively lifted her up and carried her to her front door. Luke held it open for him as he shuffled past and walked straight upstairs to his flat. Once inside, he set Emily on his sofa and went to the bedroom where he pulled out a pair of sweatpants and a t-shirt from his dresser. He could have gone back downstairs to grab something for her to sleep in, but he wasn't about to leave her alone.

After setting the clothes in the bathroom, he walked back to the living room and found Emily sitting on the edge of the cushion. She lifted her head to him as he made his way back to her. "Hey. I put a change of clothes in the bathroom for you. Do you want to take a hot shower? It will help you warm up."

"Yes," she told him.

Liam took her hand to help her stand and guided her to the bathroom. "I'll be right here in the living room. If you need anything, I'm right here."

As Emily stepped through the bathroom, she turned and quietly called his name, "Liam?"

"Yes?"

"I can trust you, right?"

God, she was killing him. Liam wanted nothing more than to run to her, wrap her in his arms, and kiss her fears away. He walked to her, her gaze lifted as he approached. Liam leaned against the doorframe to the bathroom and took one of her hands in his. Energy danced and tingled in his palm. "Yes, Em. I promise. You can trust me."

Emily squeezed his hand while looking him in the eye. She stepped closer to him. "I'm not going to lock the door. Just in case it shows itself again while I'm in here. I don't want you to be locked out."

"Okay. If you're comfortable with that. I would never do anything to hurt you." Liam kept his voice low and soft. He leaned down farther and placed his mouth near her ear. "But just so you know, that little flimsy lock isn't going to do shit to stop me from getting to you if you need me." Liam watched as a small shiver traveled down her body. Seeing Emily's physical response to his words caused a chain reaction within him. The smoldering flame in his belly grew, and he'd be damned if he was going to attempt to smother it.

When he lifted his head, he caught her eyes. They were no longer wide with trepidation. Her lids were now heavy, her face relaxed, and her breath escaped in a long exhale.

"Okay. I'm leaving it unlocked. I'll feel better knowing you can get here easier."

Liam raised her hand to his mouth. Turning it, he kissed her palm. "Go on, baby. Have your shower and get warm."

Emily stepped back, smiled at him while giving him a quick glance through her long lashes, and closed the door.

***

Emily inhaled the thick, warm steam that filled the bathroom. She stripped and climbed in the shower, adjusting the water to as hot as she could handle it. The spray stung her skin at first, but after a minute, her body acclimated to the temperature change, and she allowed the hot water to pound against her stiff muscles.

Emily had never been so cold in her life. Shaken to her core, her body was frozen from the inside out. The only comforting thought was Liam. She had been afraid of telling him what she had been living with her entire life. She was more afraid of him experiencing what was tormenting her, afraid he would think she was too much of a burden. But he didn't pull away from her. Instead, he comforted her, surrounding her in a blanketing light of caring and understanding. It was a warmth of emotions she had never experienced before. Making her feel not only safe and excepted but strong and determined—to fight the evil that had followed and attached itself to her. Liam was an anchor, holding her steady in a raging ocean of uncertainty.

Emotions flooded, sweeping over her in choppy waves, holding her beneath an undertow of current, and she couldn't bring herself to the surface. Terrified, confused, and fed up, a burning need to find answers and figure out what was happening lit itself within her. In the past, Emily walked through life…numb. She wandered through time in a haze of existence, not truly feeling or being aware of her surroundings, or her wants and desires.

She was done. An evil spirit afflicted her life with fear, and she wasn't going to allow it to continue. Wasn't going to allow it to tear her away from a man who she felt so connected with, who she knew was just as aware of her heart's deepest desires as she was. The link she felt tethering her to Liam overwhelmed her entire being, and she refused to give in to the pressure of the haunting. She was going to fight the evil that tormented her and live her life. Free.

Twelve

Liam paced his living room while listening to Phil's phone continue to ring without an answer once again. He left yet another message at the tone, this time not caring to hide the frustration in his voice and hung up. Sitting in the lounge chair next to the oversized sofa in his living room, Liam interlaced his fingers and rested his chin against his hands, elbows on his knees, he stared across the room toward the bathroom where Emily was taking a shower.

The kiss they shared on her sofa in her flat was everything he'd imagined it would be. Everything he'd remembered from his dream. The feel of his mouth on hers felt like heaven. Even the soft sigh that escaped her lips was familiar to him.

Liam pulled the chain on the lamp sitting on the side table, illuminating the room in a warm glow, before picking his phone back up and calling the one person in the world he knew would understand his predicament.

"Hey, son. How are you?"

At the sound of his father's voice, Liam dropped his head and took a deep, cleansing breath, trying desperately to hide his emotions. He knew his father would know something was up otherwise. He always did. "Hey, Dad," Liam said, his voice shaky.

"What the fuck is going on, Liam? What's wrong?"

The sound of his father's voice washed over Liam, and he smiled. "I'm fine, Dad. I promise."

"You're not fine. You're calling way later than what is typical of you. And by the sound of your voice, you're completely freaked out about something. Now talk."

Clayton Wesley was not one to be messed with. He loved his family hard and did everything in his power to protect them.

"Okay. So. Let me start at the beginning."

"That's always a good starting point, son."

"Yeah. So… I met a girl. She's beautiful. Amazing. She moved into the flat below mine a couple weeks ago."

Liam briefly filled his father in on everything that had been going on. When he got to the details about what had happened in Emily's flat, his dad was not only concerned but also angry.

"Listen, Liam. I know what you're feeling. When we were going through that crap in Sacramento, and we came home to find your mother at the bottom of those stairs, I wanted to kill somebody. Something that we couldn't see touched my wife and almost killed her. So, I know the anger you're feeling right now. But I'll tell you something else. Back then, we didn't know or have the information and technology and resources of today. This is what you do, son. You find the answers, and you help people. You need to keep your head straight. Don't let the anger overtake you. That's what the damn thing wants. It wants to ruin you. God, I wish I could've called someone like you guys back then. I can't tell you how many fights your mom and I went through. Over stupid shit. The littlest things would set us off. These things feed off of fear and anger. Don't give in to it."

Liam knew his dad was one hundred percent right. But like most things in life, it was easier said than done.

"I know, Dad. I'm just trying to figure out why the hell all of this started when she moved in. I'm not blaming her. I'm just trying to put the pieces together. What is it about her that woke this place up?"

A moment of silence hung in the air before his dad spoke, "There's something you're not telling me, Liam. I can hear it in your voice. What is it?"

Of course. His father could always read him, even over the phone. He had a sixth sense for those things. Clayton always knew when any of his children were holding something back.

"Dad." Liam paused for a moment, trying to find the right words. Realizing there wasn't any easy way to explain, he said, "She's the girl I've been dreaming about since high school. She's the one in my nightmares."

Another beat of silence followed. Liam heard his father blow out a breath. "Are you kidding me?"

"I'm one hundred percent positive it's her."

"You have Trey and Luke working on this with you?"

"Abso-fucking-lutely. They're downstairs right now covering up Emily's broken window, and they are staying the night in her flat."

"Good. Where is Emily?"

"She was really freaked out, so I brought her to my flat. She's taking a shower. And before you go there, nothing has happened between us yet."

A roar of laughter filled Liam's ear. "Yet, huh?" his father repeated. "Son, when are you bringing her out here to meet us?"

"Soon. I hope." The thought of his parents meeting the woman literally from his dreams made him happy and nervous all at once. He'd only just met Emily, but he knew she was special. Everything in him screamed that they were meant to be together. Liam pushed the fact that he'd only just met Emily aside, and focused on how his blood rushed through his body, and his heart ached when he thought of not being with her.

"Alright, listen to me. You need anything, you call. I don't care what time it is. You call! Lean on Trey and Luke. They have your back. And you bring that girl out here to meet your mom and me. Remember what I've always told you."

"I will. Thanks, dad." Liam put his phone back down. His mind kept drifting to the window in Emily's apartment blowing apart. He couldn't shake the anguish of her being hurt had she been standing near it when it shattered, exploding into tiny shards of glass. What if she'd been alone when it happened? What if his friends had been hurt?

The team was used to investigating dangerous locations. Sometimes, they were miles away from any medical services. It was a risk they took on every job, willing to put themselves in danger to help others and get answers. But he still worried about his friends. And now, Emily too. She had never dealt with the haunting being violent. She said herself that she had always complied with it. Avoiding any physical relationships with men, which seemed to keep it at bay. What if *he* was the catalyst for the violence unfolding? It was an idea that twisted Liam's gut, and at the same time, the need to protect Emily took hold.

He felt relief now that his father knew what was going on. Even if he couldn't provide any answers, just knowing that his dad understood his worry brought him comfort. The sound of Emily turning the doorknob on the bathroom door pulled his attention to the hallway. She walked out, skin flushed from the warm shower, hair damp, and his clothes hung loose on her. She was a sight of pure beauty as she made her way to him. The closer she came to him, Liam noticed the slight puffiness and redness around her eyes. He was about to stand and go to her when her steps picked up, and she threw herself in his lap. "What's wrong?" Liam asked.

Emily shook her head. "Nothing. I just had to break down for a minute."

Liam tightened his hold on her waist. Her front plastered to him, she straddled his lap once again, like she had during their kiss.

"I'm not giving in to it anymore," she whispered. "I'm done giving it what it wants. I'm not going to run from it anymore. I just don't know where to begin to fight it."

Liam shifted, placing his palm against her cheek. He gently nudged her back, keeping her close, but looking her in the eye. "You won't fight it alone. You have *me*. We have Trey and Luke to help, and we know a lot of people in the field who can help. We will do whatever it takes to get rid of it."

"Thank you," Emily said. She closed her eyes and Liam leaned forward, resting his cheek against the side of her head.

"Can I get you anything?" he asked her.

"No. I'm okay."

"Wait for me right here. I'll be right back."

Emily scooted to the side and settled on the sofa as he stood and went to his bedroom. He quickly changed into sweatpants, pulled the comforter off of his bed, and carried it to the living room.

He walked straight back to Emily. "What are you doing?" She looked up as he approached the sofa.

Liam sat next to her, unfolded the comforter from around his arm, and guided her back to lie next to him. Her back to the sofa, her front pressed to his side, the energy between them danced. "I'm not leaving you alone tonight. Not even to sleep." Liam stroked her damp hair, pushing it away from her face. "Get some rest. Tomorrow, we'll talk to Trey and Luke. We're going to take this one day at a time. Tomorrow, we'll start working on a plan of action.

Emily relaxed, and Liam felt her give him more of her weight. "Liam?"

"Yeah?"

"Do you feel it too?"

Liam tightened his arms around her and squeezed his eyes shut. "Feel what?" he asked, as his heart raced at the implication of her words. Was she feeling the same extraordinary sensations when their skin touched as he was?

"I don't know how to describe it. Whenever we touch, there's a burst of energy. A current. A pulsing. I can feel it leave your body and enter mine. Do you feel it too? What is it?"

Liam blew out the breath he had been holding. His body trembled with the confirmation that she, in fact, was experiencing the same sensation. "Yeah, baby. I feel it. Does it scare you?"

"No!" Emily stated, lifting her head to look up at him. "It doesn't scare me at all. If anything, it's…comforting."

"I don't have answers, but my gut tells me it's because we're connected somehow. I don't know how yet. But I'm going to find out."

Emily nodded and rested her head on Liam's arm once more, pushing herself closer to his body as if she were trying to cocoon herself. Instinctively, Liam pulled the comforter up closer to their chins. He wrapped his free arm around her waist, allowing her to snuggle deeper into his embrace.

"I'm sorry our first dinner together was ruined by a pissed off ghost," Emily quipped.

Liam's body erupted in laughter, and when he looked down, Emily's warm smile greeted him. "Hey, at least we'll have a great story to go along with this date." Liam kissed the top of Emily's head, and within minutes, she relaxed and took long, rhythmic breaths, indicating she had fallen asleep.

Liam lay awake for a long while, thinking. The need to find out who she was overwhelmed his instincts. His intuition told him it was the piece of information that held the answer to why she was in his dreams.

Thirteen

Emily stirred to the sound of movement. The soft cushion and smooth microfiber feel under her, alerted her senses. The warm blanket that covered her smelled of spice and musk. A momentary feeling of dread crept over her before she remembered where she was.

She had spent the night with Liam, on his couch, curled up into him under his lofty blanket. His essence now covered her from head to toe. The memories of Liam embracing her through the night swept over, and she smiled at the thought. Only now, she was alone.

The delicious aroma of coffee hit her nose, awakening her senses. Opening her eyes, the view of Liam's flat welcomed her. It was masculine, but comfortable. The enormous oversized sofa took up much of the space. Most of his furniture was a shade of grey or brown, giving the flat a warm feel, and a large flat-screen TV was mounted on the wall across from where she lay.

She sat up to the image of Liam walking toward her, carrying a cup of coffee. Although he had already gotten dressed, Emily was half tempted to ask him to crawl back on the couch with her. She had enjoyed lying across him, listening to his heartbeat against her cheek. She had also grown more accustomed to the electrical charge that pulsed between them.

"Good Morning," Liam said, his eyes sparkled. "I made some coffee."

"Mmm. Good Morning," Emily said before looking up and taking the cup of coffee he handed to her as he sat down. "Thank you." She inhaled the heavenly, nutty, slightly spicy scent before taking a sip. The luscious, smooth liquid warmed her throat and insides. "This is perfect. How did you know how I like my coffee?"

Liam chuckled. "Well, I didn't want to wake you, and I saw that Lexi had sent you a text. I didn't want her to worry. I hope you don't mind. I told her you were still sleeping and that you would text her back as soon as you woke up, and I needed to know how you like your coffee. Cream until it hits a caramel color and a bit of sugar."

Emily stared at Liam in awe. She had been attracted to him from the first moment she laid eyes on him. But now, knowing he cared about her so much that he asked her best friend how she took her coffee so he could have it ready for her when she woke up had Emily falling for him faster and harder. The more time she spent around Liam, the more he impressed her, and the more comfortable she became. "You asked Lexi how I like my coffee?"

Liam grinned, and a hint of pink bloomed across his cheeks. "Are you mad at me?"

"No, I'm not mad. That was sweet of you. Thank you."

After a moment, Liam cleared his throat. "So. I was thinking, if you're up for it, we can go downstairs so you can shower and change. Then, I want to take you to breakfast. When we come back here, we'll talk to Trey and Luke to see if they captured anything last night. Does that sound okay?"

The thought of returning to her flat had Emily's anxiety creeping up. She had decided to fight the spirit and take control of her life, but that didn't mean she wasn't scared of what he could do to her.

Liam must have caught the apprehension because he asked, "What is it?"

Emily looked up into his calm crystal eyes and said, "I don't really want to go back to my flat. I especially don't want to shower there. Just the thought makes me feel so uneasy."

Liam placed his palm on her cheek, scooting closer to her in the process. "Em, I'm not going to let anything happen to you. I'll sit in the bathroom with you until you're done if you want me to. Either way, I'll be waiting for you in your flat until you're ready. Or, if you'd like, we can go grab you some clothes and you can get ready here."

Thinking for a moment, taking in Liam's kind words, Emily answered, "I'd like to grab some clothes and come back here to shower."

"Okay. Let's go." Liam took her hand and led her through his front door and down the stairs.

"Are Trey and Luke still here?"

"No. They said they were going out for breakfast. We'll all meet back here later."

Inside, the flat was still cold. Trey and Luke did a good job covering up the front window using a tarp they had kept in the van, but it did little to keep out the morning chill.

Liam followed Emily into her bedroom while she grabbed clothes. "Em, grab enough stuff for a couple of days."

Emily stared at Liam, confused. Liam turned to face her, taking both of her hands in his. "I don't want you staying here alone until we figure all of this out. I'd like you to stay in my flat with me if you're okay with that."

"I'm okay with that," Emily said in a low whisper. And she *was* okay with it. Not only was she okay, but the relief she felt was overwhelming. Liam let go of her hands as she turned toward her closet to grab a small duffle bag. Emily stuffed the bag with a pair of pajamas and sweatpants, a pair of jeans, a pair of her favorite yoga pants and leggings, a sweater, a couple of shirts, an extra bra, her favorite warm fuzzy socks, and a hand full of panties. Then, she made her way to her bathroom and grabbed only the bare necessities, including makeup. Emily knew she could always come back to her flat if she needed anything, but the truth was she really didn't want to step foot in her flat again. At least not for the time being and definitely not by herself.

"Ready?" Liam asked from the kitchen. He was looking over notes that Trey and Luke had made.

"Yes…Wait." Emily was more than ready to leave and head back upstairs, but she couldn't forget her computer. She grabbed the laptop from the kitchen counter, the charging cable, and her planner, and placed them in her bag as well. "Okay. I'm ready."

Taking the duffle bag from Emily's hand, Liam led her back to the front door, where she put on her favorite pair of Toms shoes and grabbed a cardigan and scarf that were hanging on a hook with her purse. She grabbed them, and Liam led her out of her flat and back up the stairs. Inside, Emily let out a long sigh.

"Okay?" Liam asked.

"I think I held my breath the whole time we were in there. It doesn't feel the same. It feels different."

Liam nodded after she spoke, agreeing with her. "Heavy."

It wasn't a question as much as it was a confirmation. "Yeah," Emily agreed. "Why doesn't it feel like that here? It's the same building. How can my place feel like that and it's only a few feet away?"

Liam shook his head and stepped closer to her, where he placed his palm on her cheek. Emily closed her eyes. She now craved the grounding sensation that blanketed her every time they touched.

Leaning down, Liam placed his forehead on hers, and she could feel the heat radiating off of his entire body. "I can't give you an answer as to what is happening or why it's happening. But, I can tell you that I will do everything I can to try and get to the bottom of this and keep you safe. I just need you to trust me. Trust Trey and Luke, too. Okay?"

"I've never had anyone to lean on before," Emily explained as she tried to control the hitch of emotion in her voice.

"That changes now. You can lean on me. Me and the guys lean on each other. That's how we operate. We're a team." Liam's hand went to the back of her neck. His other hand rested firmly but gently on her hip.

"Are you saying I'm a part of your team now?"

"I'm saying you're with me now. And since you're with me, that makes you one of us."

"I'm with you?" Emily asked. Liam's declaration shot through her like a lightning bolt. Scaring her and exciting her all at once.

"Yes, baby. At least I want you to be. If that's what you want too. I know we just met. But ..." Liam paused, squeezing his eyes shut before opening them again. "I feel like I've known you my whole life. You're not someone new to me. I don't know how that's possible, but it's true."

"I'm scared, Liam. What if it tries to hurt you to keep us apart?"

Liam gently quieted her by placing a finger over her lips. "I'm not scared. Remember, this is what I do. I chase ghosts for a living. But I don't want to be with you because of everything that's happened. I want to be with you because I like you. Because the moment I laid eyes on you that first night, I felt something. Electricity struck me that moment, and now I feel tethered to you. That might scare you. Fuck, it scares me. But I'm an honest man, Emily. I'll always tell you what I feel. And what I feel for you is like nothing I've ever felt before. I don't think the English language has words yet to describe what I feel. I want you here, if you want to be here, ghosts and all. I want to get to know you. All of you. I even want to meet Lexi. So yeah, babe. You're with me. If you want to be."

Swallowing hard, Emily closed her eyes and leaned into him. "I want to be with you."

"Thank god." And with that, he moved the hand that was on the back of her neck to her chin, moving her gaze up to look at him. "Trust me, Emily."

"I trust you."

Liam lowered his head and placed a kiss on the corner of her mouth, letting his lips linger for a moment before stepping away and saying, "Go on, babe. Go get ready. I'll wait for you, and then we'll go. I'll feed you, and we can talk. Yeah?"

"Okay. That sounds good."

Emily walked into the bathroom, shutting the door and leaning against it, steadying herself. How could one man make her so weak in the knees? She felt like flowing molasses. Being near Liam caused her to slip further and further, inching her closer to a yearning and desire she had no idea existed within her. She was hungry for it, desperate to feel passion with another person, to share a closeness with someone, a bond she thought could only exist in books and movies. And for the first time in her life, she wasn't afraid to take that leap and experience the excitement and satisfaction and possibility of, dare she say, those three little words.

Fourteen

Liam explained the area they were headed to was known as Lands End, located on the Western side of the city, and he was taking Emily to one of his favorite restaurants. He promised her a delicious breakfast featuring a picturesque view. They sat in comfortable silence on the car ride across the city. Liam's hand rested in Emily's hand on her lap, where she gently stroked his knuckles. And, he snuck a peek at her out of the corner of his eye every so often. It was still hard for him to believe that the woman he'd dreamt about for years was real, in his presence, and he was able to physically touch her. "I hope you're hungry." Liam broke the quiet between them. "This place serves up some hefty portions."

Emily turned in her seat, positioning her body and leaning toward him a little more. "I am. We didn't end up eating last night. I'm starving."

Liam's jaw tightened as he remembered their dinner being interrupted by the spirit the night before. He raised Emily's hand to his lips, inhaling the scent of his own soap on her skin. She'd used his body wash when she showered that morning, but her own natural warm, vanilla scent came through and calmed his nerves. Emily allowed her hand to linger on his cheek as he turned the car into the parking lot.

Liam parked in the small lot before turning off the engine. He jogged around to Emily's door and held it open for her. Her eyes fixated on the view in front of them, and she gasped as she stepped out onto the gravel. To Liam's delight, it was a clear morning. Though there was a heavy chill in the air, the sky was clear, and not a cloud or a hint of fog was in site.

The parking lot overlooked a cliff where old ruins of concrete pools and the foundations of buildings sat. Liam tracked Emily's gaze as her eyes fixated on the historic site. "What is that?" Emily asked.

"Those there," Liam said as he pointed down toward the abandoned remnants, "are the old San Francisco Sutro Baths. They were huge saltwater pools that were a very popular hangout in the late eighteen hundreds and early nineteen hundreds. They burned down in the nineteen sixties. This is all that's left of them." Liam walked closer, standing directly behind her. He leaned down, resting his cheek next to her ear, and wrapped one arm around her waist. Using his free hand, he pointed straight out in the distance, drawing her line of sight to the pointy peaks jutting out of the ocean. "Those islands way out there are the Farallon Islands."

Emily gazed out at the ocean and took a deep breath, as if she'd never get another chance to smell the ocean breeze. "We got lucky," he told her, "You can only see the islands on very clear days."

Liam stared at her for a moment, relishing in her beauty, soaking in the sight of her. Her skin glowed in the morning light. "You haven't ventured out here yet, have you?"

"No," Emily replied. "Not yet. It's so beautiful. I'm from Seattle. I've seen the ocean before. But I've never seen it like this. I feel so peaceful here. Like I...belong." Emily turned around. Her eyes caught the glow of the rising sun behind them.

Liam put an arm around her shoulder and guided her toward the restaurant. "Come on, Em. The view from inside is just as amazing."

The hostess sat them beside a window at Liam's request. There were a few people inside, mostly at the bar having coffee. The place was quaint. It could feel cramped if crowded, but it was cozy and intimate. With windows lining most of the walls, the ocean was visible from anywhere you sat in the restaurant.

When the waitress came over, she poured them both coffee and took their orders.

"I'll have the Eggs Benedict, please," Emily told the waitress.

"And I'll have the Chicken and Apple Sausage and Eggs, scrambled, with a side order of French toast."

The waitress assured them she'd be back shortly with their food and hurried off.

Emily stared out the window, fixated on the breaking waves. "I've been feeling so stressed and worried. It's amazing how different I feel now just being here."

Liam knew all too well what she meant. Not only had he and his team helped so many people living with the stress of hauntings, but, as a child, he had experienced the same stress as well. "I know. When you live in a place that's haunted, it's good to get out as often as you can. Being away from the fear and oppression can help your sanity."

"Is that why you come here? Because you find it so peaceful?"

Liam smiled. "That is exactly why I come here a lot. In fact, when my parents retired, they bought a home down the coast in Carmel. Right on the beach. I love staying down there. It's beautiful."

"It sounds like it. I wish we could spend the day here. I haven't spent time at the beach in ages. The thought of going back to the house makes me so anxious."

Emily's words had Liam's heart jumping into his throat. He

wanted to spend more time with her, away from the house, where they could talk and not be interrupted. "We can spend some time here at the beach if you want."

"I thought the guys are waiting for us to get back."

"They are," Liam stated as he pulled his phone from his pocket and sent Trey and Luke a text that he and Emily would be back later that afternoon. "There. I just told them we would be back later. Don't worry. I promised them I'd bring home lunch. And they need time to go over footage and audio from the cameras they had rolling last night. That takes time, and we would just be bored and anxious waiting around for them at the house to finish."

"That sounds wonderful. Thank you."

"For what, babe?"

"For helping me. For not freaking out. For not trying to make me think I'm crazy and need to be on medication. And most importantly, for excepting Lexi and not being intimidated by her." Her lips tipped up in a smile at her last statement. They both chuckled.

"You're welcome, Em."

Liam was about to reach for Emily's hand but was interrupted when the waitress returned with their orders. They ate their meal while sipping on another cup of coffee. After Liam refused to let Emily pay for her breakfast, he placed some bills on the table before heading out of the building. They walked out into the salty, breezy sea air. Liam took Emily's hand, guiding her down the hill to the sand.

***

They walked along the beach, hand in hand, before finding a nice spot to relax in the sand. Neither of them spoke at first. They sat silent, holding each other's hands while watching the waves roll onto the shore and retreat.

There was something so familiar about Liam. Emily barely knew him, yet she felt like she'd known him her entire life. It wasn't common that you could sit with a person in silence and not feel awkward. But with Liam, it felt natural. As if they had been together their whole lives and were content just being with each other.

The sound of the waves rushing onshore lulled her into a deep state of relaxation, easing the anxiety that had been building since arriving in San Francisco. Emily glanced at Liam. The man was a living God. His blue eyes sparkled as the sunlight bounced off of the water. His lightly tanned skin, accented by dark stubble framing his face, glowed. And she was still in awe of the idea that Liam wanted her. A thought that caused her insides to flip and tingle all at once.

He stared out at the ocean, and she sensed he was grappling with a thought. She leaned toward him and said in his ear, "Penny for your thoughts."

Liam looked over at her and smiled. He leaned back on an elbow, stretching his legs out in front of him. Looking back out at the ocean. "I'm thinking about this girl."

"Aw. A girl, huh?"

"Yeah. I haven't known her for very long, but she's starting to work her way into my heart."

Whoa. She was not expecting that. Liking the little game he was playing, Emily decided she would play along. "Work her way into your heart, huh? Interesting. Well, judging from that blush on your cheeks, I take it that's a good thing and not a sign that she's annoying you."

"She could never annoy me." Liam shook his head while he drew circles in the sand with his finger before looking up.

"Oh, you would be surprised. Especially since you don't know her very well. People have a way of nitpicking the little things after a while. You might find that you hate the way she chews. Or the way she lets her clean laundry sit in the basket for days without folding it."

"That could never happen." Liam chuckled. "I happen to know for a fact that I love watching her eat. I also happen to know that I couldn't give a shit about where she puts her clean clothes."

"Well..." Emily leaned back on her elbow. The wind was calmer closer to the sand, and the sound of the rushing waves surrounded them, blocking out all other noise. It felt as if they were the only two people on the beach at that moment. "What if she has a crazy friend who is super overprotective?"

"Then, I'd be glad she had an amazing friend who cared about her."

"What if she lived in a haunted house and had been followed by ghosts her entire life who were *dead* set on keeping her from finding happiness?"

Liam gently tugged on her arm, and she scooted closer to him. They were so close if they'd been any closer their eyes would have lost focus. Liam stared deep into her eyes, his own gaze fierce but protective.

"I don't care about haunted houses. I would promise to help her find out what was following her and put a stop to it. Ghosts don't scare me. That's why I hunt them. There is one thing that scares me. I'm afraid to tell her because I don't want to scare her."

"What?" she asked him with concern in her voice.

Liam cupped her cheek with his palm and pulled in a deep breath.

"I've had haunting dreams myself for years."

"You have?"

"Yes." Liam stared at her. He was still struggling with the thought in his head. Emily watched as his jaw clenched, and his lips pressed together.

"Tell me?" she asked as she placed her hand on his cheek in an attempt to comfort him. She knew the fear of having reoccurring dreams and not understanding them. Understood the anxiety of wanting to confide in another person but being afraid to tell anyone.

Liam closed his eyes and took a breath. When his lids opened, and his gaze met hers, he said, "In it, I'm surrounded by a man. I can't move because I've been hurt. But that's not what scares me."

"What scares you?" Emily whispered.

Swallowing hard, Liam continued, "There's a woman in my dream. Always the same woman. She's been hurt and held captive. I can't move and I can't help her."

"Oh, Liam." Emily moved closer. She could see the anguish he felt from thinking about it. "Why would that scare me?" Emily didn't understand his worry about scaring her. The emotion was clearly visible across his beautiful face. He spoke again.

"Because that woman is you."

Emily pulled away a fraction and looked into Liam's eyes. She could see the concern in them. His lips still pressed tightly together, his hand squeezed hers. Deep down, she knew he wasn't lying. He was confiding in her the way that she did with him. "How can I be in your dream? We only just met."

Liam shrugged and shook his head. "I've been trying to figure it out, and I've been terrified to say anything to you because I don't have an explanation. All I can tell you is that I've seen you in my dream since high school. I've always hated having it. Now, I almost want to dream it nightly so I can figure it all out. But I can't, and it's driving me crazy. The second I saw you that night outside of your flat, I knew who you were. The beauty from my dream. The one I can't get to.

"That morning, when you saw the shadow in your bathroom, I heard you scream, and I had a flashback to my dream. It's the same scream. That's why I ran downstairs so fast. I had to get to you. I know down to the marrow of my bones that somehow you and I are connected. Please tell me, you know of me too."

Emily closed her eyes and put her forehead to Liam's. "In my dream, everything is hazy. The images aren't clear, but I can hear you. I can hear your voice. It's you. I know it's you I hear."

"Really?" Liam moved his hand to the back of her neck, pressing their foreheads tighter to one another.

"Yes. I was going to tell you last night while we were talking. It's your voice I hear in my nightmare, calling for me. Only I can't see you. But, we started talking about the shadow, and then Trey and Luke showed up. I know we are connected. I knew it the moment we both had that vision yesterday in the hallway. I do feel it. It should be scaring the hell out of me, but I'm not scared. I want to be with you, and I want to find out what is happening too."

"You're sure?"

"Yes," Emily told him firmly.

"I think we need to start with finding out your past. Who your birth parents were. It might help us understand what is going on if we know who they were. Are you okay with that?"

"Yes. I don't want anything to do with them, but I'm okay with trying to find out who they were."

"When we get back, I'm going to tell Trey and Luke about it, and we'll start researching."

Emily gave him a nod. "Alright. Liam?"

"Yes?"

"What do we do now?"

Liam smiled at her and moved his hand to the back of her neck, bringing her closer to him. "I'll tell you what we do, babe. We're going to try and just be as normal as possible. Yeah, we have some crazy shit going on, but we're still human, and it's quite obvious that we're attracted to each other. So, we're going to do what all newly dating couples do. We're going to sit here for a while longer and make out like two crazy teenagers until I'm satisfied that I've memorized every inch of your beautiful mouth and lips. Then, we'll walk back to the car. We'll grab lunch for all of us then head back to the house. We'll walk into your flat holding hands and give those two dipshits something to talk about behind our backs until they corner me and beg me to tell them how I convinced my hot new neighbor to go out with me."

"Wow. You have that all planned out, don't you?"

"Yep. And I expect you to give Lexi a call and tell her the news. Tell her I'm not going anywhere. I'm not going to be scared away."

"I can do that. And, please, don't call your friends names. They're not dipshits."

Liam chuckled. "Don't worry, baby. It's all in good fun. You're right. They are far from being dipshits. They're friendly dipshits."

Emily burst out in a belly laugh that she couldn't control. It felt good to let go and forget and just…be. Liam joined her in laughing. After a minute, when they both calmed down, Emily looked at him again and said, "Right. Friendly dipshits. Oh boy. I'll never be able to look at them again without thinking that."

"Good," Liam said, still grinning from ear to ear. "Take out your phone."

Without questioning why, she handed it to Liam when he held out his hand for it. He opened the camera app and put it on selfie mode. "Smile," he said. Emily leaned close. They were now cheek to cheek, smiling and looking happy. Liam took the picture and sent the photo to himself before he handed it back to Emily. "Send that to Lexi. I'm assuming she's at work and won't be able to call you for a while. That will keep the wheels in her head turning all day until she can talk to you."

"That will. And it will drive her insane."

Liam laughed again. "I expected as much. I have a feeling me and her are going to get along really well."

"Yes. You two definitely will." Emily sent the photo to her friend with only the caption of…
Emily: Hey, Lex. Love you lots. Call you later.
"And one last thing, Em."
"Yes?"
"I'm probably overstepping my boundaries here, but it's how I feel. I was serious when I said I don't want you to stay in your flat. I want you safe in my flat with me. I'll sleep on the couch. You can have the bedroom. But there's no way I'm letting you stay alone in that house with all of this shit happening. Not until we get it under control."
"Liam Wesley, are you asking me to move in with you?"
"Yep. At least temporarily. When this shit is over, we can talk more about living or sleeping arrangements."
"Sleeping arrangements?"
"Oh yeah, babe. Sleeping arrangements." He said again with a grin.
Emily laughed, still in shock at Liam's request that she stay with him. She felt more relief than apprehension that she wouldn't have to go back to her flat. Liam obviously cared about her. He'd even offered to sleep on his couch and give her his bedroom to make her feel more comfortable. "Okay. I'll stay with you until this blows over. Now, are you going to kiss me? Or are you going to keep stalling?"
"I'm not stalling. I'm working up to the perfect moment."
"Oh, really?"
"Yeah, really."
And with that, he closed in on her, his lips on hers. Heat seared through his hands and into her skin. Her blood pounded in her ears. The energy between them became magnetic—two polar opposites pulling, grasping for a thread to hang on to. Emily had no idea she could fall for a man so hard and fast. She went against every wall, every barrier she ever put up around herself, and let her energy collide with his, sealing the magnetic bond.

Liam did exactly what he said he would. He took her lips gently, but after a while, Emily let his tongue in, and they dueled with each other, tasting and exploring until they were both breathless. Eventually, she felt Liam pull back, and he moved to her neck where he nibbled on the sensitive skin by her ear. "We should get going." His breath was hot against her flesh and her skin pebbled with excitement.

"Yeah. We probably should. We wouldn't want to make too many people jealous," she told him with a giggle as his kiss tickled her neck. "We have a little audience," she continued and nodded to the side where there were some passerby's averting their stares.

"Good. I don't care if they're jealous. What are they gonna do? Have me arrested for making out with my girlfriend?"

Emily laughed and Liam moved his mouth back to hers, placing feather-light kisses across her lips and cheek.

Fifteen

"Tell us what you found last night." Liam stated as he placed a sandwich on a plate.

Luke sat at the dining table, the small, wooden chair creaking under his muscular weight. "Nothing, man. It was completely quiet. We didn't pick up anything on video or the recorders during the night."

"Strange that it was so quiet after all of the activity you two witnessed." Trey sat next to Luke, and Emily was next to Liam settled across the table from them. They were all big men. Even sitting down, they took up much of the space in the dining area. Yet, Emily felt comfortable and at ease surrounded by them.

The three friends talked about which cameras they planned on using that night during the full investigation. Emily listened in wonderment as Liam spoke with his teammates about the plans for the evening. Although she didn't understand everything the three best friends discussed, she was amazed at how they could each guess what one another was about to say. They were all passionate about their work. Speaking with enthusiasm, each one gave deep thought to the ideas being tossed around. Emily was fascinated. She was a fly on the wall in her own apartment, and that didn't bother her in the least.

Emily was still lost in her thoughts when Liam grabbed her attention by placing his hand on hers.

"I'm sorry. What?"

"You really spaced out there," he said as he leaned forward in his chair.

Emily stared into his calm, blue eyes. "I'm sorry. Just daydreaming."

Liam scooted closer in his chair and whispered, "You get enough to eat?" He indicated to the half-eaten sandwich still sitting on her plate.

Emily nodded. "I did. I'll wrap it and take it upstairs and finish it later." Trey and Luke had made their way back to the kitchen to clean their plates.

"I'm about to tell the guys about what we discussed at the beach. Is that okay?"

"Yes." Emily squeezed Liam's hand.

He squeezed hers back and replied, "It's going to be alright. Trust me?"

"I do."

Trey and Luke were at the sink washing their plates when Liam suggested they go to the living room.

Trey and Luke walked out of the kitchen. "We found your vacuum, Emily, and we cleaned up the shattered glass. I think we got it all," Trey told her.

"Yeah. We lifted the couch cushions and vacuumed under them too. But still, be careful. You probably want to vacuum a few more times. Just to be safe," Luke added.

"Thanks, guys. You didn't have to do all of that. I really appreciate it,"

"Let's go sit in the living room and talk." Liam kept Emily's hand in his as he stood up from the table and led her to the sofa. Trey and Luke followed behind them and settled in the two chairs across from Emily and Liam.

"So, Emily and I talked today," Liam began. "I told her about my reoccurring dream. Both of the beating and of her. She also knows about my past experiences with the paranormal while growing up."

Trey and Luke nodded in approval. After a beat, Liam continued.

"Here's the thing. Emily has been tormented her entire life by this haunting. It follows her. It's not a possession, but it seems like some kind of an attachment."

Intrigued at Liam's statement, both friends sat forward.

"We didn't get to tell you last night because of everything else that went down. We need to dig into Emily's past. Maybe there are some possible clues as to why she's been followed. But, Emily doesn't know who her family is because she was abandoned at birth. Left at a fire station in Seattle. She was raised in foster care."

"What?" Trey said, surprised.

"God. Emily. We're so sorry." Luke said.

"It's okay," Emily said. "I've made peace with it. Like I told Liam, it used to bother me. But over the years, I decided that I didn't want to go through life pissed off at people I didn't even know." Emily took a deep breath. "If Liam thinks finding out who they were can connect the dots and tell us why this haunting started, then I'm on board with it."

"Emily." Trey stood from his chair and walked to the table where his laptop sat. "Were you ever told anything about the woman who dropped you off at the fire station? Anything at all? What she looked like maybe, or even a first name?" he asked as he took a seat and began typing away on his keyboard.

"The only thing I was told was that my birth mother was a drug addict. They knew because when I was taken to the hospital, they found traces of drugs in my system. I had to go through withdrawals before I was healthy enough to go into foster care. I was never told what she looked like. Only that she handed me to a fireman and walked out."

"Okay," Trey said and wrote down everything Emily had stated.

Luke then spoke up, "Emily, do you know the fire station where you were left? That might help us."

Emily gave Luke the station number. She stayed quiet for a while. The two men busied themselves with typing away on their laptops. Liam sat with his arm around her waist and held her close. She felt safe. For the first time…ever.

Liam whispered in her ear, "This is what they do. They are great at gathering information."

Emily smiled at him and nodded. Then, he cleared his throat, breaking the silence in the room. "Guys, I was thinking of having Emily join us tonight during the investigation."

Trey and Luke looked up with questions in their eyes.

"I think it's a good idea. There was no activity in this house before her arrival. Not that any of this is your fault." Liam's eyes hit hers, and she was thrown into a vision. Her hearing muffled, and a blurry image clouded her sight, just like the one she'd seen in the hallway the day before after she and Liam returned from their date. Emily's breath caught. She blinked rapidly. Forcing the image from her head. Liam was back in front of her."

"You okay," he asked her. His features dropped in concern, and she felt the pressure of his hand around her waist tighten.

"Yes," Emily breathed out. Her heart thundered, and she was sure Liam could see the movement of her arteries in her neck. His gaze shifted to the spot right under her ear momentarily, before coming back to her eyes.

"I'm not saying any of this is your fault," he told her. "You've been tormented your whole life, and we are going to find out why."

"I know. I'm fine. I wasn't expecting you to suggest I investigate with you." It was true, his statement had caught her off guard, but she would wait until they were alone to tell him what really caused the blood to pulsate through her body.

Emily relaxed against Liam, and he continued. "It seems like things happen most often and are the strongest when she's present," he said as he looked to Trey and Luke. "So, having her with us might bring whatever this thing is out. Plus," Liam brought his eyes back to Emily, "you're a photographer and are comfortable with a camera. Maybe if you're the one snapping pictures, we'll capture something."

Luke nodded in approval, "I get it. That is a good idea."

Trey added, "I agree. But only if you're one hundred percent okay with it."

Liam turned to Emily. "I know we haven't discussed it yet. I just thought of it. If you're okay with it, I think it's a good idea. You'll be with us the entire time. We are not going to leave you alone."

Emily nervously played with her hands in her lap while she toyed with Liam's idea. Her first thought was that she didn't want to be part of the investigation. Then she changed her mind when she considered how long she had been dealing with being haunted. A moment of determination struck her, and she once again reminded herself that she was done. Done being scared, done with always being on edge, done of pretending to be okay with the fact that she was not happy.

"I'm one hundred percent on board with it. I want this to end. I don't want to wonder from day to day what will happen, or what will follow me whenever I move. Or, when I'll have another dream. I want it to end."

Liam brushed her cheek with his thumb. "Then, we will start tonight with getting to the bottom of it."

Trey and Luke had gone back to their research. Liam stood and took Emily's hand. "Guys, we're going to go upstairs and talk about how tonight will go. Let's also get some rest before tonight. I'll order dinner around 4:30. We'll get started not long after sundown."

"Sounds good. We got it," Luke replied.

Once upstairs, Liam kept hold of her hand and gently turned her so her back was to the closed door. Emily reached her hands out and grasped his waist. He leaned down close to her. His breath warmed her skin as he spoke. "What happened downstairs?" his voice was low, etched with worry but still held a sexy undertone that sent tingles through her.

"I had a vision," Emily blurted out. "It was just like the one in the hallway yesterday. I think it's you, but it's not clear. You looked at me, and I instantly fell into it."

"I'm sorry," Liam whispered.

Emily's brows knitted. She reached her hands up, one going to the back of his neck, the other rested on her cheek. "For what? For looking at me? Please don't stop. No one has ever looked at me the way you do."

Liam stepped closer to her and bent his knees to keep his face near hers. "How do I look at you, Em?"

"Like..." She thought for a moment, searching for the right words. "If I walked away, you would break into a million pieces."

"Good," he told her firmly. "That's exactly how I feel. I won't stop looking at you. Now I know the warning signs. If I see your eyes go blank like that again, it means you've slipped into a vision. Do I have your permission to kiss your gorgeous lips to help bring you out of it?"

Emily nodded. She couldn't help the smile form as her skin turned hot from his words. "Yes. You have my permission." Before she could get another word out, Liam's mouth crashed onto hers. This time, he kissed her fiercely, as if he were claiming her as his own. Emily's heart pounded in her ears as desired filled her, and her knees went weak. If not for Liam's weight pressing her against the wall behind her, she was sure she'd collapse.

His mouth left a trail of burning, moist kisses down her neck, where he settled his lips at her collar. "Liam?" He brought his mouth back up to hers and nibbled on her lower lip. "We should talk," she told him with a gasp.

He lifted his head, his eyes dark with desire, and his heavy breathing matched hers. "I've never..." Emily began, her eyes fell to the floor.

"Emily, look at me." Liam used his finger under her chin to direct her stare back at him. "You can tell me anything. I'll never judge you."

"Things are moving quickly between us. I'm okay with that. I've never wanted to be with anyone as badly as I want to be with you. I just need to tell you. I've never..." Emily's words trailed off again as her heart rate sped into overdrive. Liam brought his hand to her face and smoothed her hair back. "I'm a virgin," she whispered and threw her head back against the door. Emily closed her eyes, not able to meet Liam's gaze.

She felt his lips brush her cheek gently and make their way to the corner of her mouth. "It's nothing to be embarrassed about," he told her.

"It's weird, I know," she said in a long breath.

"What?" Liam said, shocked.

"Liam, I'm thirty-two years old and a virgin. It's weird," Emily stated.

"No, baby. It's anything but weird. Unusual, maybe. Weird? Not at all. You said you dated that dipshit phycologist, and I just assumed—"

Emily held her hand up to stop him. "We dated for a few weeks. He was the first serious boyfriend, if you want to even call him that—"

"I'm not calling him that," Liam interrupted.

Emily laughed before continuing, "He was the first guy I considered to have been a boyfriend. I never dated in high school. And in college, I went on a couple of dates but nothing ever serious. Every time I was interested in someone, all of the activity around me would pick up. So,

I would just forget about it and go about my life. I never slept with the phycologist. I never wanted to. I'm not saving myself for marriage or anything. I just haven't found the right person. Until…now."

Liam took her hand and led her to his sofa. He settled them both much like he had the night before, on their sides, with Emily's back against the cushions. Her front pressed against his front, and her head cradled in his arm. "We'll go as slow as you need to. I'm not going to pressure you. Just having you here in my arms feels like heaven."

Emily relaxed, letting out a long breath. A few moments passed before Liam spoke again. "Are you sure you're okay with tonight?"

She lifted her head to look at him. "I am. Truthfully, I don't want to be alone. I'll feel better if I'm at least near you guys. I'll admit, I'm nervous as hell, but I want to know what is going on. And like you said, if this thing is focusing around me, maybe me doing the investigation with you three will help get answers faster."

"What about trying to find your birth parents? Are you still okay with that?"

"Yeah. I'm okay with finding out who they were. But if we do locate them, I don't want to talk to them."

"Don't worry. Me and the guys will figure something out. If you don't want to see or talk to them, then you won't have to."

"What will happen tonight?" Emily asked as she lay her head back down.

Liam tightened his grip around her and said, "It will take a bit to get set up. We'll set up different cameras and make sure everything is working right. Then we'll go over a plan of action as to how to start. We'll show you how to use the full spectrum camera. I just want you to take pictures. If you feel something or have an urge to take a photo, take it. We'll let you know if we need you to take a photo of a particular spot. It will be very dark. We investigate in full darkness, but we'll have night vision cameras so we can navigate. Just stay close to me. It will be okay."

"Alright. I can do that." Her breathing had finally calmed, and she yawned. "I'm so tired."

"Sleep. We have a long night ahead of us. Let's take a nap. When we wake up, we'll eat and get started." Liam grabbed the comforter that he'd left from the previous night and covered them. Within minutes they were both asleep.

***

Pictures flashed in his consciousness, taking him back to the night when his ability to make choices freely was stripped, trapping him within the walls of a home once belonging to him. He had chosen to stay behind, but it was the seeing woman who cursed him, confining him to the building.

Over the years, he had grown stronger. Using his power to see outside of the confines of the house. When he sensed the aura of his love returning to the Earth, his ability to subconsciously travel allowed him to keep watch. Only something consistently worked against him. It held him back, keeping his grasp on her, yet at the same time, just out of reach.

Now, she had returned and was in his territory, where he was strongest. He would have her. Eventually, she would fully belong to him.

Sixteen

"So basically, the full spectrum is just a modified camera that allows for more UV and IR light to pass through and allows an image of a spirit to be captured."

"Right," Emily held her hand out to Liam. "It looks just like a regular point and shoot camera."

"It is." Liam placed the camera in her hand. "It has an SD card and a fully charged battery. But, I'll give you this." He picked up a large fanny pack and unlatched the buckle. Liam guided the straps around Emily's waist and connected the two ends, adjusting the straps so it sat comfortably on her waist. "There are extra batteries and SD cards in here. Sometimes on investigations, spirits will drain batteries from electronics and mess with the way they work. If that happens, switch out whatever you need, and we will question it later.

"Alright."

"I think we should start here at Emily's since this is where the most activity has happened," Liam announced. They all agreed, and when Luke returned from making sure all of the lights were off in the building, they got started.

Just like on every other investigation, Liam took the lead and began asking questions using the EVP recorder.

"Tell us your name?"

"Why are you following Emily?"

They used almost every piece of equipment they had during the first few hours. Nothing showed up on thermal. The motion detectors remained silent. And no disembodied voices had been picked up.

Frustration crept up on Liam. After everything they had experienced recently, it was discouraging to be three hours into an investigation and not have any evidence.

Because there hadn't been any strange activity in Liam's flat on the top level, the team decided to focus their energy in Emily's flat and the basement. With the lack of evidence, Trey suggested that they try splitting up, each of them taking a different area of the building. Trey was now in Liam's flat, and Luke was in Emily's.

"Okay, now it's pitch black down here," Liam said to Emily as they descended the stairs to the basement. "I have the night vision camera so we can use that to see where we are going. Stay close and hang on to me."

"Don't worry," Emily responded. "I'm not letting go."

It wasn't only the shaky tone in Emily's voice that gave her nervousness away. She had a death grip on Liam's waist, her fingers digging into his sides. The heat from her hands seared through his shirt and imprinted on his skin. Sparks of electricity traveled through her hands and into his body. Her grasp was so tight, he was sure she would leave marks on him.

Liam commended her for sticking around and assisting them a few times already. Most people couldn't handle being in pitch blackness knowing a location was haunted. He was damn proud of her courage and determination.

Liam guided Emily down the wooden stairs, into the bowels of the building. The stale scent of the concrete foundation and walls hit him. His eyes watered at an unfamiliar dank odor that he'd never smelled before. His senses screamed at him that something was off. Years of experience told him to stay alert. If he blinked, he might be taken off guard.

Liam kept his eyes trained on the screen of his night vision camera as he asked, "How are you doing?"

"I'm fine. I just hate it down here, and with the lights off, it's even worse."

He felt Emily step to his side. Her hand remained on his waist. "If it gets to be too much, let me know," he whispered to her. "We'll stop and take a break."

Emily squeezed his waist a bit harder when she replied, "I will."

Liam normally never paused in the middle of an investigation, but this was Emily's first time doing any kind of paranormal work. He'd only sprung the idea of her joining them earlier that day, and he wasn't about to push her, especially after everything that had happened to her recently.

As they rounded the bottom of the stairs, Liam felt Emily stop abruptly, halting his forward movement. "What is it?" As soon as the words escaped Liam's lips, he felt it. An intense instinct to run washed over him, and it took everything he had to tamp down his fear so as not to alarm Emily. Even with all of the years of investigating under his belt, he couldn't help his body's natural reaction to tense.

"Something is here with us. We're being watched."

"I feel it too." Eyes were watching them. Liam couldn't see where they were, but he felt them. Piercing glares bared down on them. A fuzziness came over him. A hazy fog clouded his mind, and he couldn't think clearly. Each thought increased his exhaustion level.

Liam knew it was the entity's way of trying to control his emotions, and he pushed the fear down and asked Emily to begin another EVP session.

Emily held up the recorder and spoke.

"Is anyone here with us?"

Silence.

"What is your name?"

Silence.

"Where are you from?"

While Emily asked questions, Liam continued to scan their surroundings through the night vision camera's viewfinder and guided Emily through the basement's darkness.

"It's cold," Emily said. Her voice shook with a shiver.

"Yes, it is. It wasn't this cold a minute ago." Liam moved the camera around some more and froze at the image on the viewing screen. He reached for his walkie talkie, held it up to his mouth, and spoke to both Trey and Luke. "Guys, can you read me?"

Luke responded first. "Yep. Whad'ya got?"

"Do we have anything to break this lock on the apartment door? I also need an EMF detector. Somethings down here with me and Emily. I swore I just saw a mist go through the locked door."

"Copy that," Luke replied. "I'll grab one and bring it to you. As for the lock, we weren't able to get anything to break through it today. I don't know if we have anything in the van. But I'll take a look."

"Copy that." Liam placed the walkie talkie back in his pocket and looked over at Emily. The air was cooling rapidly, and she was shivering.

"Hey, sweetheart. Let's take a break. We'll go help Luke out in the van."

"Okay." Emily turned slightly toward the stairs, anxious to leave the dark subterranean room. "I could use some fresh air."

"Okay. Let's—" A loud bang cut Liam off. Both he and Emily jumped, and he hugged her to his side. Emily's breathing sped, and his own heart threatened to break through his chest. "It's okay," he whispered to her. "I've got you. Let's get out of here. I'll figure out what that was later."

Liam guided Emily toward the stairs, and they walked up together. Halfway up, a blast of cold wind rushed through them, nearly knocking both of them backward. Emily dropped to her knees, and Liam managed to swing himself around and crouch on the step behind her, making sure she didn't fall any further. A frigid tunnel of icy wind swirled around them. The bitter chill making it difficult to take a breath. Liam grabbed Emily by the arm and hauled her upstairs as fast as he could.

When they reached the top landing, he yelled, "Trey!"

A moment later, Trey was running down the stairs from Liam's flat. "What the fuck happened?" Trey asked when he made it to Liam's side.

Liam stood in front of Emily. Her chest moved rapidly with each laborious breath as she leaned against the wall. Her hands grasped his upper arms. Liam leaned over her, caging her between his body and the wall.

Liam lowered himself and placed his forehead on hers while he spoke to Trey. "We were in the basement. We felt a tremendous temperature shift. That's when I radioed to you guys that we need to get into this locked room. We decided to come back up because it was becoming too much for Emily. Then, we heard a loud bang, we booked it up the stairs. We were halfway up when a fucking cold breeze—No, not a breeze, a fucking whirlwind—went right through us. Almost knocked both of us back down the stairs."

"Shit," Trey mumbled. "Let's get her outside."

Liam nodded in agreement. "Give her a minute first. She's really shaky."

Emily looked up at Liam, eyes wide and pleading. "Get me out of here."

Without another word, Liam wrapped his arm around her shoulder and led her out of the house and down the steps to the parked van in front. Luke was already aware of them rushing down the steps and helped Emily into the back of the van. Trey followed close behind. He carried a blanket that he'd grabbed from Emily's flat and handed it to Liam.

Liam settled Emily in front of the monitors in the back of the work van that the team used as headquarters while on investigations. He grabbed a jacket that he always kept handy and put it on. Hoping the lightweight fabric would ease the chill he felt still coursing through him. A few feet away, Liam heard Trey filling Luke in on the activity that had just taken place.

"What was that?" Emily asked.

"My guess is that something doesn't want us down there," Liam answered. His voice carried a bit of enthusiasm. He couldn't help the giddiness take over. Whenever contact was made with a spirit, the rush always shocked him at first, followed by a thrill of excitement. His only regret was that Emily had been with him, and she was now frightened by the activity. He reminded himself that the occurrence was a good thing, despite the fear that it caused. He had recorded the mist he'd seen in the basement on the night vision camera. He was also sure he'd caught the moment when he and Emily had almost been knocked down the stairs. Their job was to gather as much evidence as possible and use it to help rid people of hauntings. They had accomplished that. Now, they just needed to figure out who or what the entity was and how to detach it from Emily. "Something wants to keep us away from that locked room."

"But we aren't giving up, right?" Emily stared at Liam with bravery. "We're still going in. Can we break the lock to find out what the fuck is hiding out in there?"

Liam heard both Trey and Luke chuckle behind him. He couldn't help but smile at Emily. "Yes, we are. But not tonight. After what just happened, I'm not taking any chances with pissing it off any further until we find out more about what we are dealing with. There will be another investigation soon." He told her while leaning forward, taking in her sweet scent. "I'm going back in there with Luke to finish up. Trey will stay here with you. You'll be able to watch us on the monitors."

"I really want to go with you. But I don't think I can just yet."

"I know you do. You stay here and get warm. Trey will make some coffee."

Emily glanced around, her brow furrowed, confusion clearly visible on her face.

Trey stepped into the van and pulled a small portable coffee maker out from one of the shelves.

"We always make sure we can brew coffee anytime, no matter where we are." Liam said as he pulled Emily close to him.

"It's hard to get coffee in the middle of the night, and sometimes our investigations are in remote places." Trey plugged the coffee pot into a power strip that ran to the main power in the house. He grabbed a bottle of water and a bag of coffee from a crate that also held a supply of coffee cups and powder creamer.

"Wow. You guys are really resourceful."

Liam placed a kiss on her lips. "I need to make a phone call. Are you okay by yourself for a minute?"

"Yes, I'll be fine." She smiled at him and kissed him back.

Liam stepped out of the van and pulled his phone out of his back pocket. He swiped it open and sent a text message. A moment later, a ping notification sounded, and he pressed his dad's speed dial number.

"Son? What's going on?"

"Hey, Dad. I don't have a lot of time to explain, but I was wondering if you and mom are around this weekend. I need to be somewhere where I can think clearly and know Emily is safe. I want to bring her down to Carmel for a few days. Longer if I can convince her."

"We are in town. Don't plan on going anywhere. Especially now that I know you two need a safe house."

Liam chuckled at his father's statement.

"Head on down here as soon as you can. Are Trey and Luke coming with you?"

"I don't think they need to come. I don't want to—"

"Bullshit?" Liam's dad interrupted. "You bring those boys with you. You know your mom would love to see them. It's quiet here. Your mom and I spend most of our days on the beach anyway. Bring everyone down. You guys can work, and Emily will be safe here. You'll have a larger support system while you research."

Liam knew it was no use arguing with his dad. Once Clayton Wesley made up his mind, it was set in stone. "Okay, Dad. I'll talk to everyone later, and we'll head down in a couple days."

"Good. You have the spare key. Don't worry about calling before you arrive. Just head down when you can. See you soon."

"Thanks, Dad."

Liam ended the call. It was time to make this investigation a priority. This haunting had already proven itself to be dangerous. The question was, why now? And where and how did he and Emily fit into all of it?

Seventeen

The drive down the coast was beautiful. Emily stared out the window and watched as they drove along an endless stretch of the coastline. The sky was blue, and a blanket of grey lay out on the horizon, waiting for the sun to set before it inched its way back to hug the land, creating an interesting contrast while shadows from the clouds danced on the ocean below.

It had taken Liam some time to convince Emily that time spent away from the house would do both of them some good. She was nervous about meeting his parents. But, Liam explained that he needed to be in a place where he knew she was safe, away from the flat where the activity surrounding her seemed to be the strongest. And, somewhere he could think more clearly while he and the team completed their research. After hearing him out, Emily agreed. Maybe it would be good to get away from the stress of the haunting for a while. She just hoped it didn't follow her to his parents' house.

Trey and Luke were making their way down the coast as well. Liam assured Emily that his parents' house had more than enough space to accommodate everyone. Though she was still nervous, the thought of maybe getting a peaceful night's sleep outweighed her apprehension. She hadn't slept for more than a couple of hours at a time since arriving in San Francisco. The lack of sleep was beginning to wear her down.

Emily turned and looked at Liam. His arm rested across the center counsel, his hand holding hers in her lap. His other hand gripped the steering wheel. "You doing okay?" he asked her.

"Mmhmm. I already feel so much better. Relaxed."

Liam smiled at her and raised their hands, kissing the back of hers. "Good. Still nervous?"

Emily wrinkled her nose. "A little. Isn't this strange? We've only just met."

Liam chuckled. "Baby. My parents are not the conventional type. They were engaged a month after meeting. And eloped a few weeks later."

"You're kidding." Emily's eyes widened.

"Nope. They've always said they knew they were meant to be together the moment they laid eyes on each other. So, trust me when I say, you really don't need to be nervous. They're excited to meet you." Liam brought her hand up to his lips. The feel of his breath lingered on her skin. "You have nothing to fear. They love having company and practically begged me to bring Trey and Luke. So, no worrying, okay?"

"Alright." Emily exhaled and shifted her body, resting her head more comfortably in the seat.

"Sleep, sweetheart. We have about another hour or so before we get there," Liam told her. And she did.

Emily slept and didn't notice when Liam had pulled the car to a stop and turned off the engine. She woke to Liam stroking her cheek, "Em, we're here."

Her eyes fluttered open. She squinted as they adjusted to the warm, bright sunlight. "Hey."

"Hey," he said. "You ready to go inside? It doesn't look like anyone is home right now. They've probably gone into town for lunch and a walk. Let's get settled. I'm sure there's food in there to fix for lunch. Trey and Luke should be arriving shortly."

The house was breathtaking. Views of the Pacific Ocean were visible from almost every room. One end of the home was dedicated to the master suite next to an office, and the other end of the home had four large guest rooms with the two wings separated by an open concept main living space. The enormous room was connected to the dining room and a gourmet kitchen. And to top it off, a beautiful garden lined the front of the home, welcoming guests to the property. Emily could imagine all of Liam's siblings, nieces, and nephews visiting and the house being full of laughter. That thought made her smile.

"What are you thinking about?" Liam pressed his front to her back and wrapped his arms around her waist. He rested his head against hers, and she breathed in his spicy scent as she nuzzled against him. His beard scratched against her temple.

"How beautiful it is here. Thank you for bringing me."

"You're welcome." He kissed her neck before taking her hand and leading her back toward the hallway. "Come on. Let's go get our bags and get settled."

Liam carried the large bags while Emily carried her small bag with her laptop. He stopped in the hallway to turn and asked, "Do you want to stay in a room by yourself? Or do you want to share a room with me?" Surprised, Emily blinked as she looked at him. Liam put down the bags and stepped toward her. "I want nothing more than for you to stay with me in the same room. But, I know things have been chaotic lately, and that's why you've been staying with me. I don't want you to feel obligated. If you want to stay with me, I'll be relieved because I'll get to continue holding you every night. But if you want to stay in your own room, I'm perfectly okay with that."

Reaching for his face, Emily kissed him and said, "I want to stay with you. I know things have been crazy. And as weird as it sounds, I'm glad things have happened because it brought me to you. If you don't think your parents will mind, then, yes. I want to stay with you."

"I'm glad too." Liam placed another kiss on her lips. "They won't mind. Like I said, they are not traditional." Liam was interrupted by the sound of the front door and in walked Luke and Trey.

"You guys got here fast."

"Yeah. Traffic wasn't bad today. Where's mom and pop?" Luke asked.

Liam's parents had pretty much adopted both Trey and Luke as their own. They weren't only mom and dad to their own children. They were mom and dad to all of their children's close friends.

"Probably in town on a walk. And don't go begging my mom to cook you up a feast when she gets here," Liam warned.

"Why not? She'd be happy to cook for us," Trey cut in.

Liam looked at his friend and shook his head. "Dad said they stocked the fridge and pantry for us. We can fix something to eat while they are out."

Trey already had his head in the refrigerator, and Emily could only stand back and listen to the hilarity of the conversation. It was all she could do to not laugh out loud.

"We're in luck!" Trey shouted. "Mama Wesley, always thinking about us," he stated while pulling out a casserole dish from the refrigerator.

Liam made his way over to Emily where she stood watching the scene unfold before her, grinning from ear to ear.

"You guys act like you haven't eaten in two days," Liam said.

"We haven't," the two friends said in unison.

"Don't worry, Liam. I'm happy to take care of you boys," a voice said from behind them.

Liam turned and greeted his mom in a warm hug. "Hi, Mom."

"Hi, sweetheart. How are you?" Janet Wesley hugged her son tight. She was around Emily's height, just over five feet, and she was indeed a beautiful woman. With barely a hint of makeup on, she was stunning and wasn't afraid of her age. That was evident in the natural grey hair that she wore proudly, accenting the strands with honey and blonde highlights, allowing them all to blend together and set off her blue eyes.

Emily could see the resemblance in Liam to his father, who was also tall. Both men slightly resembled Adam Levine. Only they both had more hair and Liam definitely had his mother's sapphire eyes.

"I'm good. I missed you."

Luke was quick to come up next for a hug. "Hey, Mama."

"Hi, honey." Then it was Trey's turn.

"Mama. You look beautiful, as always."

"Aw, thank you. Did you boys find the casserole?"

"Yes ma'am," both Trey and Luke answered, then moved to Liam's dad for handshakes and hugs. When everyone had finished greeting each other, and his friends turned their attention back to the casserole, Liam took Emily's hand and brought her to his side.

"Mom, Dad, I want to introduce you to Emily. Emily, my parents, Clay and Janet."

Emily held out her hand. "It's very nice to meet you, Mr. and Mrs. Wesley. I've heard so many wonderful things about you."

"Oh, my dear," Liam's dad spoke up, "we are not formal people. You just call us Clay and Janet. It is very nice to finally meet you," and he pulled Emily in for a hug. Then, Janet wrapped her arms around Emily and whispered, "If there is anything you need, anything at all, don't be afraid to ask. Okay?"

Emily felt tears burning in the backs of her eyes and tried to blink them away. She nodded and felt Liam pull her to his side once more.

Emily was thankful when Janet pulled the attention away from her by inviting everyone into the living room while she warmed up the casserole. Simultaneously, Liam's phone buzzed, and he pulled it from his back pocket to answer it.

"This is Liam...Yes...Say that again, please."

Liam rubbed his brow with his hand. His head dropped down as he walked to a barstool at the kitchen island and took a seat. Emily's heart sank. She had no idea what the call was about, but she guessed it wasn't good judging by Liam's drastic change in demeanor.

"I don't understand. Are you sure...? Okay...Yes... I am out of the area for a few days. As soon as I get back, I'll call you. Okay.... Thank you."

"What was that about?" Trey asked.

Liam ran a hand down his face. "That was Phil's lawyer. Apparently, Phil passed away." His voice hitched, and emotion filled his eyes.

"What?" Shocked, Emily made her way to Liam, putting her arms around him. She held him while he rested his head on her shoulder. His breath warmed her neck as he breathed deeply against her.

After a few moments, Liam lifted his head and stared into her eyes. "That's why I couldn't get ahold of him."

Emily held his face in her hands. "I'm so sorry."

"There's more. Phil named me as his next of kin. He left me the property."

The next few moments were filled with, "You're kiddings" and "What's?"

Emily spoke, "This is becoming more and more complicated."

"It is. There is something we are missing, and I hope we come across more clues soon. There is nothing we can do about it right now. We need to focus on one thing at a time right now. We will enjoy our time here, and when we get back to San Francisco, I'll meet with the attorney and get all of the details. Until then, we are going to use these next few days like we planned. Relax, research, and plan our next investigation."

***

The next morning, Emily woke to the gentle brush of Liam's breathing on her shoulder and the smell of coffee and bacon. For a brief moment, she considered skipping breakfast, wanting to snuggle next to Liam for as long as possible. But, the growling in her stomach protested that idea. She gently slipped out of bed, careful not to wake Liam, and padded her way to the bathroom before heading to the kitchen. "Good morning."

Janet was busy at the stove, frying up the delicious bacon. A cast-iron skillet sat on a trivet on the counter. The smell of a frittata wafted and mingled with the scent of the bacon

"Good morning, dear. Coffee?"

"Please. It smells amazing."

"Thank you. I don't get to cook like this too often anymore. I love it when the boys come to visit. I can cook all day long and not have to worry about freezing leftovers." Janet smiled as she spoke.

"You're a wonderful cook. And I love your gardens. They're beautiful." Emily stood at the kitchen window while staring out of the bay window facing the front of the house.

"Thank you. Feel free to go out anytime. It should be a nice day today. The fog pack has pulled back already. It may be chilly, but the sun is out."

"Thanks. I think I'll do some work out there. I'm used to the chill. I'm from Seattle. I'm definitely going to soak up some sunshine."

"Seattle?" Janet asked her. "Clay and I have been up there a few times. It is beautiful. What brought you down this way?"

Emily took a sip of her coffee and placed the mug on the counter in front of her. "I don't really know. It's hard to explain. I woke up one day and felt like I needed a change. I got on the internet and started looking for rentals in San Francisco. I didn't know why San Francisco called to me, but it did, and I fixated on it. I came across the flat, and it was listed for an amazing price. It was very spontaneous. I'm normally not that impulsive with decisions. But it felt right."

Janet sat at the barstool across from her at the kitchen island after finishing up the bacon. She padded the stool next to her, inviting Emily to sit. "You trust your instincts. That's good. Obviously, you're here for a reason. I'm a believer in fate. Everything happens for a reason. I know you're going through some difficult times. Clay has filled me in when Liam has called him. I've been there. Let me tell you, it gets worse before it gets better. I think you're here because you and Liam need each other. It's obvious there is a connection between the two of you. You guys will figure it all out when the time is right."

Emily wasn't expecting such an in-depth conversation with her new boyfriend's mother so soon. She felt at ease and comfortable talking to Janet. Something she wasn't used to but welcomed the experience.

"Janet, do you mind if I ask you a personal question?" Emily turned to face her. Janet's ocean blue eyes were just as intense as Liam's. Warm and welcoming.

"Sure. Go ahead."

"Liam told me about the house in Sacramento."

Janet nodded, "I expected he would. What would you like to know?"

"How did you deal with it all? The anxiety? The fear? Not knowing what would happen from one moment to the next? I've been dealing with something my entire life, but it's never been this extreme. I've always been able to ignore it. But, this time is so different. I'm scared it's trying to break up Liam and me."

Janet set her own coffee cup down and reached for Emily's hand. She held her in a firm but comforting grip. "Never give it the satisfaction that you've given up. You said it's been with you your entire life. Let it know that now it needs to leave. It doesn't have control over you. You and Liam are meant to be together. Just like Clay and I. The love we had for each other and our family, that's what held me together. I wasn't going to let any damn ghost ruin my family, and neither was Clay. Know that you're not alone in this, either."

"Thank you, Janet. You know, I've never had a family. You've made me feel so welcome, and I just want to say Thank You. For accepting me."

"Of course, honey," Janet stood and threw her arms around Emily. "You know what you remind me of, Emily?"

Emily shook her head.

"An Anemone."

"I'm sorry?"

Janet smiled warmly and sat back down. Emily sat with her, eager to hear what she was about to say. "An Anemone. It's the Greek word for a Windflower. They are delicate but strong. They sway in the wind, but they keep standing tall. When a rainstorm moves in, they close up to protect themselves and open back up again in the sun. And the wind will pick the petals off the flowers and carry them away. I believe the cosmic winds plucked you up and led you here to Liam. You keep standing tall and strong. You'll get through this. Both of you will pull through. You'll see. You're not going to let some psycho spirit run you down. If you need anything, you just call. Promise me."

"That's right." Both women turned their heads to see Liam's dad standing in the kitchen with them. He strode over to Janet and put his arm around her waist.

"How was your run, honey?" Janet asked as Clay placed a sweet kiss on his wife.

"Great. That's right, Emily. You call if there is ever anything that you need."

"I will," Emily promised.

"Something smells delicious," he told Janet while pouring himself a cup of coffee.

"I made a Frittata."

Clay's eyes widened as his brows rose. "I'm digging in before those boys wake up." Clay grabbed three plates from the cupboard.

"Oh, I made plenty, Clay. Don't worry."

Emily watched as Clay dished up three healthy servings of the frittata and handed her a plate. "You're not alone in this, Emily. You're important to Liam. He cares for you. Trust him. He and the boys have been doing their jobs for a long time. They've seen a lot, and they know what they're doing. They won't stop until they get to the bottom of what is going on."

Janet walked over to her husband and said, "You know, you're the only girl Liam has ever brought home?"

Shocked, Emily lowered her head, slightly embarrassed. "Uh. No. I didn't know that."

"It's true. Even in High School, he never brought a girl home. Oh, he went on plenty of dates, but never did he bring anyone home for us to meet. You, my dear, are one special girl."

Tears welled up in Emily's eyes then, and she couldn't help them from spilling over. Clay walked around the island and took her in his arms just as Liam walked into the kitchen.

"What the hell, Dad? You makin' my girl cry?"

Liam stocked over to Emily and took her in his arms. "It's okay, Liam. Your dad is very sweet. I'm sorry. I'm just really emotional lately. I'm not upset. I'm grateful. No one has ever made me feel so welcome before."

Janet and Clay had made themselves busy in the background setting the table and making more coffee when Janet said, "Come on, everyone. Let's have some more coffee and eat."

"Are you hungry," Liam asked. His hands gently cupped her cheeks.

"Yes. I want to finish my plate. Your mom is an amazing cook."

"Yes, she is."

Eighteen

"My gut's telling me there's a lot more going on here." Clay sat in the leather lounge chair in the office. His hand stroked his chin while he thought.

"Yeah, we know." Trey looked up from his laptop that he'd set up at Clay's desk.

"I'm hoping once I meet with the attorney, we'll be able to find some more answers." Liam and his friends had gathered in the study, and his father had joined them to discuss the haunting and Phil's passing.

"Liam," Trey continued to stare at his computer screen. His eyes moved rapidly, reading the information in front of him. "I think I found something."

Everyone stood and made their way to him. Liam stepped into the hallway and called for Emily. Moments later, both Emily and Janet walked into the study.

"I found this news article. It's about a man who mysteriously took possession of a home after his business partner's death," Trey told everyone as he turned his computer around. "Liam, the home is your address."

"You're kidding," Clay said as he and Liam leaned closer over Trey's shoulders.

Liam read the article. "It says, Robert Banks, a San Francisco socialite, was taken in for questioning about the possible involvement in his business partner's death, Henry Mitchell. Banks was questioned due to his sudden inheritance of the home not long after Mitchell's son, James Mitchell, and friend, Abigail Quine, disappeared."

"What?" Luke said in a shocked tone.

Liam looked at Emily, who was staring at the screen blankly. "Em, baby? What is it?"

Emily looked at him, her eyes full of shock. "I'm not sure. Those names sound familiar to me, but I have no idea why."

"Liam," Trey pulled Liam's attention back to him. "That EVP we got the other night. It said, Abigail."

Liam straightened and looked into Emily's eyes. "What if Abigail used to live in the house and the spirit is referring to her?"

Trey turned in his seat and asked, "Could this spirit be Abigail?"

"No," Emily answered. "The spirit is a man. I don't know how I know, but I do. It's definitely male." Emily looked back up at Liam. "How do we find out who she was?"

Liam shook his head. "We keep digging. This is good, baby. We've needed history of the building. With this piece of information and the EVP from the other night, this may just be the piece we need to start putting this puzzle together."

Clay asked as he straighten and took a step back, "Trey, did you find anything else?"

"No. So far, just this. There wasn't enough time to research the other night. We were focused on gathering evidence after Liam and Emily caught the shadow figure on camera. We are just now able to dive into the history of the building. But it hasn't been easy. Though this information here can help us a lot."

"You boys keep me updated," Clay urged. "I want to know what else you guys find."

"We will, Dad."

"Liam, your mom and I talked to Casey. We're going to go visit her and the kids in a few days. But if you need to come back down here to get away, you guys feel free to come down. No need to call."

"Thanks. How is she doing?" Liam asked as he sat down with Emily on the large leather sofa in the study. Liam's younger sister, Casey, had been going through a rough time. She insisted all was well, but he knew—everyone knew—something was up, and he was glad his parents were going to check in on her.

"I'm hoping she'll take us up on our offer and come stay here," Janet said.

"I have some words for Mike," Clay said, his tone harsh.

"You need back up?" Luke asked.

"No, I think we'll be okay."

"Call and let us know if you need any help, Dad. We'll be there as fast as we can," Liam told his father.

"Appreciate that, son. I will. And I'll keep you posted on what happens."

"Is everything okay?" Emily asked, concerned.

"Yeah. My sister's husband is a real pain in the ass. But don't worry, Dad's gonna set him straight. How about we go rest for a bit?"

"That sounds like a great idea."

Liam guided Emily to the bedroom, where they snuggled next to each other. He couldn't get enough of the feel of her warm body next to his. He gently pushed a lock of curls off her face and kissed her lips. Emily curled herself into him, tucking her head under his chin.

"Liam?"

"Yeah?" Liam moved his hand to the back of Emily's head, holding her to him.

"I don't know why I know those names. I've heard them before. I just can't put my finger on it."

"We'll get to the bottom of it," he whispered. "It will just take some time. This is what we wanted. We needed some information, and we got it. We'll keep going about our lives. Enjoy our beach getaway and use the clues once we get back to the city. Either to help us research further or to provoke the damn thing during our next investigation."

Emily lifted her head. She gazed into Liam's eyes, and he felt the invisible strings in his chest reach out further and lock onto Emily. "Why do I feel like I know you so well?" she said.

Liam caught her mouth, kissing her passionately. They went from slow and sweet to hot and desperate in a matter of minutes. Their hands roamed each other's bodies, their teeth crashed with need. Both of them lost in an intoxicating lust.

Emily pulled back to catch her breath. Liam caught her eyes and brought her hand to his mouth, where he kissed her knuckles and palm before making his way back to the area of her neck that he knew drove her wild. The spot just below her ear. His hand found the hem of her shirt and snuck it underneath. Her skin was fire and bursting with sparks.

"Liam," she moaned his name when he removed his hand from under her shirt.

Liam lowered his head and kissed her again. "Baby," he whispered on her lips before taking her mouth once more. But before the kiss turned hot and steamy again, he pulled back. "I have a surprise for you."

"You do? What?"

"I'm taking you to dinner tonight."

Emily's eyes widened with delight, but Liam caught a hint of apprehension.

"What's wrong?" he asked.

"Nothing, I just didn't bring anything nice to wear."

"Don't worry. We aren't going anywhere that fancy. Jeans and a sweater will be just fine."

"Okay." And this time, Emily kissed him and made it very clear that she didn't want to stop. But now wasn't the time. There was no doubt that Liam wanted Emily. If he was being honest with himself, he wanted her from the moment he saw her. The thought of making love to her overwhelmed his senses. But he had made up his mind that he was going to take things slow.

"Em," he said as he pulled back. He felt her body stiffen under him, and he shifted his gaze. "Look at me?"

When her eyes met his, he continued. "Have no doubt that I want you. I want you more than I have ever wanted anything in my life—more than I want my next breath. But right now is not the right time. When we make love for the first time, it's going to be slow. And it's going to be where there aren't any nosy ears close by to hear you scream when I make you come over and over again."

Emily's eyebrows rose with his last statement, a crimson hue began to creep up from her chest to her cheeks. The knowledge that he could cause such an intense and immediate reaction to her senses made his dick twitch with excitement. Liam knew that probably made him sound like an asshole, but it was the truth. And he damn sure wasn't ashamed of the reaction she caused his body in return.

"That's right, Em. Over and over. I'm gonna take my time with you and make sure you know how much you mean to me. I'm positive you're it for me. I don't want anyone else. We've been in each other's dreams for a reason. We're supposed to be together. I'm not proposing marriage to you yet, but I want you to know that I am serious about us. Once all of this shit is over, I hope we can focus on where the future takes us both, together."

"Wow," Emily breathed as she stared up at Liam.

"Does that scare you?"

"No. It doesn't. I'm ready to move on with you and... *live.* I've been hiding my entire life. I'm done. Whatever this thing is, I'm ready to fight it and be done with it once and for all. And as for you and me, have no doubts that I fully intend to stay in San Francisco. I want to explore this relationship too. I want to see where life takes us. I am not running anymore. I don't care how long it takes. Even if the bastard decides not to leave me alone. I'm sticking with you. He'll just have to deal with it because I'm not letting him dictate my life anymore."

"I'm so proud of you, baby. That's the exact attitude we need to have in order to beat him. Or it. Whatever the fuck it is. We need to show it that we won't back down. Now we need to get dressed. I want to take you to dinner. I'll show you downtown. It's a nice little area. You'll love it."

"I can't wait to see it. Thank you, Liam."

"You never need to thank me, babe. Now come on, let's get going."

Nineteen

Liam had gone to meet with Phil's attorney early that morning, and Emily stayed behind in his flat. Liam had been nervous about leaving her alone, but she assured him she'd be fine. He made her promise to call him immediately if anything happened, and she agreed.

Emily was feeling more relaxed than usual that morning. Usually, a touch of anxiety always lurked beneath the surface. She still had nightmares each night, but being with Liam calmed her. He brought her…peace.

Liam's parents insisted that they stay a few extra days and take advantage of having time alone when they left to visit Liam's sister. It had been a week since they arrived back in San Francisco, and almost two weeks since Liam had taken her to dinner that night in Carmel to a quaint little Mediterranean restaurant.

Emily had never seen a town as adorable as Carmel By The Sea. The downtown area was filled with shops and restaurants housed inside of fairytale, cottage-style buildings. Emily had never been to Europe, but she felt like she was walking through a historic European village. Little alleyways of stone-paved streets meandered between and behind the buildings. Many of which had vines growing upward, covering the bricks and stucco.

They sat and ate a delicious meal of gyros, falafel, Greek salad, and hummus. Afterward, Liam took her to a nearby beach where they walked for a bit and watched the sunset. Emily couldn't remember the last time she had felt as calm as she had that night on the beach. It was as if the weight of everything that had plagued her during her life was lifted off her shoulders. Being with Liam felt so…right.

Emily brought herself out of her daydream. Her mind had drifted off to her time in Carmel while she lounged on Liam's sofa, talking to Lexi, filling her in on the last week.

"You've gotta get down here so we can spend the weekend there. You'll love it," Emily told her.

"Well, actually. I'm so glad you called today because I've been dying to tell you that I got some time off. I was thinking of coming down there and spending some time with you. I totally want to go to Carmel. I also want to go to Napa! I've always wanted to see wine country."

Liam walked through the door then. He wore a pair of dark denim jeans and a light button-up shirt that hugged his body. Emily's mouth watered at the sight of him.

Liam gave her a wink and a smile so sexy it sent shivers through her body. He walked over to her, leaned down, placed his hand over the mouthpiece of the phone, and kissed her. When he pulled back, he licked his lips, and the desire in his eyes was evident, sending the flutter she felt in her belly shooting down, exciting her. "Liam just walked in," Emily said while watching him stroll to the kitchen. She hoped Lexi didn't pick up on the elevation of her breathing.

"Tell him I say hi!"

"Lexi says hi."

Liam had poured them both some iced tea and walked back to

the living room. He placed the glasses on coasters on the table and pulled Emily close to him on the couch. Then, asked her to put the phone on speaker.

"Hey, Lexi. How are you?"

"Great. Thanks. I was just telling Em that I got some time off at the hotel. I was thinking about coming down there to visit."

"Oh yeah! That sounds great! I can't wait to meet you."

"Good. I was thinking of flying down in a few days."

"That's perfect!" Emily told her, "I'm so excited!"

"Awesome. Okay. I gotta run. My break is almost over. I'll let you know next week what day I'm flying in."

"Sounds good. Can't wait to see you."

"Take care, Lex. We'll see you soon," Liam told her.

They said their goodbyes, and Emily disconnected the call. A second later, Liam pulled her on top of him on the couch and was devouring her mouth. "Mmmm. I missed you," he told her.

"You were only gone for a couple of hours."

"Babe, you need to understand something. You're a breath of fresh air for me. I need you like I need oxygen. Being away from you is suffocating."

"Baby," Emily said and rested her forehead on his, "that is the most beautiful thing anyone has ever said to me."

"It's true."

After a beat, Emily asked, "How did the meeting go?"

He sat up so Emily could scoot back to give him room. She sat facing him, and he took one of her hands in his. "Well. It was all written down in black and white in the will. Phil left the property to me. It's all paid off, of course. He's owned this place for decades. I think it was passed down to him through family too."

"Why wouldn't he leave it to family?"

"Because he literally didn't have any. He never married and didn't have kids. He was an only child too."

"Wow." Sadness came over her. Liam leaned back, resting his head against the cushions. Emily reached her hand out to stroke his forehead. "He must have been so lonely."

"I know." Liam swiped his hand down his face and pulled Emily to rest at his side. "The attorney is having some paperwork drawn up to have the deed transferred to my name. Once that's done, it'll be official. I'll own this house."

"It's both incredible and odd at the same time."

"It is. But it's reality. I've been doing a lot of thinking these past few days. I'm considering turning this place into our headquarters. With it being paid for and the amount of work we have, I don't need a renter. We can keep our equipment stored here. Me and the guys can get the basement squared away and cleaned out. And I mean that both literally and spiritually."

Emily stared at him. She was excited for Liam and the guys to have a place for a headquarters. Then, something struck her. Liam noticed the change and reached for her. He pulled her onto his lap. She now straddled him

"Em. I've also been thinking about us. What do you think about moving in with me?"

"You want me to live with you?" Emily's heart about stopped at his suggestion. She hadn't stepped back in her flat alone since the night they saw the shadow figure. And when she did go downstairs, Liam was with her. She'd been staying with him since then, loving every moment of it. But they hadn't talked about her officially moving in until now.

"We've already been living together this past month. I know it wasn't in our plans to move this fast. But I love having you here." Liam kissed her hand before pulling her closer to him. "I was a hundred percent serious when I told you that you're it for me. I don't know how I know, but I know, down to the marrow of my bones, that you're the one I want to be with from here on out. If you don't want to move in yet, don't worry. I'll hold off on doing any renovations so you can continue living downstairs until you're ready to move. But just know, I want you with me. And I'll wait for as long as you need me to—"

"Shhhhh." Emily held her finger up to his lips, quieting him. "It's ok. I want to live with you."

"You do?"

Emily laughed and kissed Liam. "Yes! The thought of leaving you just to sleep downstairs hurts. It's weird for me because I've always been so independent, but I love being here with you. You make me feel…whole."

Liam draped his arm around her waist while his other hand went to the back of her neck, caressing her skin. "Are you sure?" he asked.

"Yes, I'm positive. What's the worst that can happen? We find out that we can't stand each other, and I move out. Though, I highly doubt that is going to happen. Sure, it's not the norm these days, but who's to tell us what we are supposed to feel and do just to appease societal standards. I want this. For the first time in my life, I want to do what I want and not be afraid of repercussions. So, damn it! That's what I'm going to do. Now, tell me what you're thinking of doing for renovations."

"I am so happy." Liam continued to caress the skin of her back while he spoke. "For starters, I want to expand this space up here. I have some ideas in my head. I need to draw them out and talk to a building engineer since this place is so old. I want to gut it. I want to add another room, maybe two. Redo the kitchen and bathroom and add an ensuite to the master bedroom."

Emily's mind swirled, trying to picture how the new space would look. "That's a lot. Where will you get the room to add two additional rooms?"

"I can reconfigure the stairway. And I want to turn the downstairs into a couple of offices."

"A couple? Why not just use the whole space?"

"Because I want you to have your own office. We can redo the kitchen, make it smaller, and build an office for you where you can work, and me and the guys will have a space to meet and work. We can even add a couple of meeting rooms where we can have clients come if they're local, so when your clients come to see you, they don't have to see our paranormal stuff."

"You would do that?" She reached up and ran her hands through Liam's hair.

"Of course, baby. I told you. I'm in this for the long haul. We're going to make this work for both of us."

Emily's breath caught. No one in her entire life, with the exception of Lexi, had ever given any thought to her needs. She had always dreamed of having a separate workspace. And now, here Liam was telling her he was going to build her one.

"Say you'll move in with me, Em. Say you'll work right next door to me, so we're never apart."

"Yes, I'll move in with you. Yes, I'll work next to you. Yes, to all of it." Emily crashed her mouth down on to Liam's lips. They made out there on the couch like they'd done so many times over the last few weeks. And like always, Liam pulled back when things became intense.

"Don't stop," Emily told him.

Liam looked at her. He was lying on top of her. One of his hands had found its way under her shirt where he caressed the sensitive skin at her ribs.

"Are you sure?"

Emily nodded. "Yes." And she reached her hands up to pull his mouth down to hers.

"Have you eaten yet, baby?" Liam asked her. "I want nothing more than to take you right now." His voice was captivating, raspy, and deep as he spoke, sending lustful shivers down her spine. Goosebumps broke the surface of her skin where his hands touched. "But, your well-being always comes first for me. I need to make sure you're fed first. Because once I have you in bed, I'm not letting you come up for air for a very long time."

Emily felt the blood flood her chest and cheeks. She knew Liam noticed the hot flush wash over her because he smiled, and his eyes lit up with more desire. "Not yet. You?" she breathed.

"Nope. I went straight to see the attorney and came right back here afterward." He looked out of the window then back to her. "It's going to be a cold, windy, and rainy day. Let's order in. Chinese okay?"

"Yeah. That's perfect."

"You got it. Put on a movie. I'm gonna grab my phone."

Emily grabbed on to him, halting his movement. "I like you right here."

"I like me here too. I'm gonna like it even more when I get you in bed and have you naked. But we need to eat first because we are going to be expending a lot of energy today. And I can't order sustenance without my phone. So, I'm gonna go get it and order food. Then, we'll cuddle here and eat, and after that, I'll lay on top of you for the rest of the day and tonight if that's what you want."

Not sure how to respond, Emily could only feel her cheeks burning more, and she knew she was bright red. "Okay, Liam," was all she could manage to say.

"Okay, baby. Here, get cozy under this blanket. I'll be right back."

Yeah, this was perfect, Emily thought before she grabbed the remote to find a movie.

Twenty

Emily was right. The movie wasn't necessary. She had found some action flick and put it on. But the moment Liam returned to the couch after ordering their food, they continued their make-out session on the sofa. It was carnal and full of want, and they both sighed and whimpered when they were interrupted by the doorbell, indicating that their food had arrived.

Liam hadn't just ordered lunch, he ordered enough food to last them the next few days. He wasn't kidding when he told her they weren't leaving the house that weekend. Emily had almost regretted eating the soup. It warmed her belly, and she started to doze off while Liam put the leftovers in the refrigerator.

When he returned to the living room, he did as he'd promised. He climbed on top of her and helped her come awake by peppering kisses down her neck. He lingered his lips above the collar of her loose-fitting sweater that provided just a hint of cleavage. It drove her mad that he wouldn't move lower. She wanted his lips on her more than she wanted to breathe, and she wiggled underneath him in an attempt to move the sweater up and expose more of her skin to his touch.

She didn't get very far in her efforts, however. Liam jumped up and stood, staring at her. Heat filled his crystal blue eyes with a fire she had never seen in them before, causing her own desire to stir deep within her even more. Liam held out his hand to help her stand. A moment later, she was enveloped in his arms, her legs wrapped around his waist, her mouth roaming his neck while he carried her to the bedroom.

Once he sat her on the bed, he said, "Scoot back, baby, and get comfortable."

She did and watched as he removed his pants, leaving his boxers on and keeping eye contact with her the entire time. Emily slid her pants down, and Liam helped her get them over her feet. Then, she pulled the sweater she wore off and tossed it to the side.

When she started to remove her panties, Liam stopped her. "Easy, baby. There's no rush," he told her.

"I'm not really sure what to do," Emily admitted, feeling self-conscious.

"Don't think about it. Just enjoy what I do with you. We're going slow. I'm going to explore you and memorize every single inch of you. Every. Single. Inch," he reiterated to her before moving his head lower to kiss her neck again. Then, lower to her now exposed breasts. He'd expertly unhooked her bra while they were on the sofa, and the short stubble on his jaw scratched her skin, leaving a delicious sensation across her flesh.

Now he was pulling the straps down her arms, freeing her breasts completely. "God. You are so beautiful," he told her after tossing her bra to the floor. Liam lowered his head farther and took one of her nipples in his mouth. Emily thought she was going to come apart right then.

Liam kissed and devoured her as if his life depended on it. "I can't get enough of you. I thought I could go slow, but I don't know if I can. You have my senses so overloaded I can't see straight." Liam's voice resonated with a roughness that had Emily's desire soaring. His grip on her hips held her in a vice, yet his mouth on her remained tender. It was a delicious contradiction of sensations that sent her head spinning and elevated her sexual appetite for him even more. "I want to memorize every curve, sound, taste, smell," he rasped.

"We have all night. And all weekend," Emily reminded between breathless kisses. She eased her panties farther down her hips again, and this time Liam didn't stop her. He helped her push them over her feet.

He reluctantly let go of her nipples and scooted up, so he was face to face with her again, kissing her passionately, before saying, "Are you okay with this, baby?"

Emily looked at him. Her eyelids were heavy with lust, and her breathing turned erratic.

"God, yes, Liam. I've never been more okay with anything."

"You'll tell me if you want me to slow down or stop. I won't be mad. I'll do whatever you need. Promise?"

"I promise. Now. Can I touch you?"

Liam smiled from ear to ear. "Yeah, baby. You can touch me all you want."

He sat back on his knees and took Emily's hands, helping her up to kneel with him. She placed her hands on his chest and felt tremors move through his muscles. His body heat seared through her palms and radiated up her arms. His eyes were closed, and it was evident he was holding his breath. "Are you okay?" she asked him.

"Yeah, I'm perfect."

"You looked like you were a million miles away."

"I'm good. I just can't believe you're physically here with me right now, not just in my dream. Where no one can hurt you. No one can take you away."

Emily let her hands slide down his rib cage and his sides, where they snuck their way to his back and under the elastic of his boxers. Liam sucked in a breath and caught her hands as they were making their way toward his front.

"What's wrong," Emily asked, hesitantly.

"Nothing, baby. But if you don't stop touching me, I'm gonna come right here in my shorts."

Emily blew out a sigh. Liam put his arms around her back, heating her skin as his hands glided over her flesh. His lips crashed down on hers, taking her in a kiss so deep her head spun as if she were drunk. Emily felt Liam move his mouth to her ear, where he sucked on her earlobe and nipped her neck. "Turn around," he whispered.

"What?" Confused and intoxicated by her desire, she wasn't sure if she heard him correctly.

"Baby, turn around for me."

Emily did as he asked her. She turned around on the big king bed, resting on her knees. Liam held her around her waist, pulling her close, pressing her back against his front. She could feel his erection pressing on her ass, and that only turned her on more. "Open your eyes."

Not sure why he was asking her to do it, she opened her eyes and quickly found the image of herself and Liam in the long mirrored closet door across the room. Her breath caught, overtaken by the sight. Liam was behind her, still in his boxers, but she was completely naked, vulnerable, and more turned on than she had ever been in her life.

"I want you to see yourself. See how gorgeous you are. Watch me worship you."

Emily's mind spun. She struggled to find words to form sentences. She stared at the mirror as the room around her morphed. Her mind played a different image. One of her and Liam, but in a different time, in the same position they were in now. The room's wood trim was the same, but everything else was different: the bed, the furniture, the light. She could even smell different scents. Before she knew what she was saying, she blurted out, "We've done this before."

"Shhhh. It's okay. I know, baby. I see it too."

"You do?" Emily gasped.

"I do. It's a vision. Stay with me, though. Stay with me. Here. In this room. Right now. Not back then."

Emily nodded and blinked, clearing the image from her mind. She found Liam's gaze in the mirror once more. "Stay with me. Right here," he repeated.

"I'll try. Promise you'll bring me back if I slip back into a vision."

"I promise. I'll always bring you back to me."

Emily turned her head toward Liam and pressed her head into his neck while his hands explored her body. She felt one hand go to her breast as his other slid down her stomach until he reached her aching core. Emily threw her head back, gasping as his fingers slip between her folds and began to tease.

Emily had brought herself pleasure plenty of times, and it had always taken her a while to get there. She had no idea that the moment Liam touched her, she would be ready to explode. It took all of her will power to hold back, wanting to enjoy the feeling of Liam's hands on her for the first time, for as long as possible.

Emily opened her eyes and found Liam's gaze in the mirror. She didn't think the image could be so erotic, but it was. Liam inched his mouth close to her ear. Feeling his hot breath against her, he whispered, "Don't hold back, baby. Let go. I've got you. Let go."

And with that, Emily couldn't hold back anymore if she wanted to. She felt every muscle in her body tighten as she arched her back. Without warning, her orgasm ripped through her, and she groaned, bucking her hips and panting into Liam's neck. If it wasn't for Liam kneeling behind her, holding her up, she'd have collapsed on the bed.

She felt him gently lower her to the mattress, where she lay catching her breath. It was minutes before she came back down, and Liam had removed his boxers. She hadn't even noticed when he'd slipped on a condom.

"Hey, you," he said, smiling down at her.

She smiled back at him. "I want you," she said.

"Trust me, baby. You'll get me. I'm not done with you yet."

He didn't bother waiting for her to respond. He simply lowered himself down her body. When she realized what he meant, Emily threw her head back and said, "Oh. My. God."

Liam took his time teasing her with his lips and tongue before driving in with full force, drawing out another orgasm from her. He kissed his way back up Emily's body and settled over her, propping himself on his elbows and waited for her to look at him.

"Are you okay?" he asked her.

Emily nodded. "Yes. Right now, I'm more than okay. But I still want you."

Liam shifted and let himself rest against her. He easily slipped between her folds, but he held himself back. Emily hitched her legs up his sides and squeezed him.

"I don't want to hurt you," he told her.

"You won't. Please, Liam."

Liam reached down and guided himself inside of her. Grabbing hold of her thigh, he hitched it higher, pushing further into her body. Emily drew in a sharp breath and felt herself slip into another memory of the two of them, in that same room once again. The vision was vivid. One of Liam making love to her, just as he was making love to her now. Emily gasped, "Liam?"

"Stay with me, baby."

"I'm here." She told him and whimpered in deep pleasure as she arched her back, her breath hitched again. Liam slid his hand down and grabbed her ass.

"I'm sorry," he breathed in her ear.

"I'm okay," she told him. "You feel so good."

"So do you."

Liam moved in and out of her body, making slow, sweet love to her.

"You feel too good. Come again." He sat up on his knees, taking her hips with him. She felt his fingers begin to play with her clit again, and before she knew it, she was on the brink of another exploding orgasm.

"Let go, baby," he coaxed through his own panting. "I'll catch you. Let go."

The sound of Liam's voice ignited a fire within her, and she saw stars explode behind her eyelids. Liam shifted, pinning her underneath him. One of his hands found hers on the bed, and he held onto her as if his life depended on it. His other arm cradled one of her legs in the crook of his elbow. He moved easily, but still slowly, in and out of her body now, sending waves of delicious pleasure through her.

Emily reached up with her free hand and laced her fingers in his hair. She knew he was holding back. And she didn't want him to. Emily wanted. No. She needed to feel his strength, his power. "You feel so good," she whispered. "I want more."

"I don't want to hurt you," he breathed out.

"I promise you won't. Please." Emily had never been one to beg for anything, but she knew if Liam didn't give her what she needed at that moment, she might die.

"Wrap your legs around my waist and hold on to me." Liam released her leg and snaked his hands under her, where he cradled her head.

Emily locked her ankles behind his back. She reached her hands under his arms and gripped his shoulders. Then, he began to move, gradually picking up his pace while he stared into her eyes.

"This is perfect," Emily whispered, answering a question she knew he hadn't yet spoken.

Liam dipped his head to her neck and sucked on the skin below her ear. She gasped. The unexpected sensitivity of his lips on her skin, combined with the sensation of him moving within her, sent pulses through her body, and she shuddered underneath him. Seconds later, Liam panted and groaned into her neck as his body shook.

Minutes passed, and they held each other while they both caught their breaths. Emily opened her eyes to Liam staring down at her. "Hey."

"Hey," she echoed, lifting her chin to kiss his lips again.

"You okay?"

"Yeah. I'm more than okay. I've never felt more alive."

"That was a lot harder than I meant to take you." Liam smoothed her hair off of her perspire slicked forehead.

"It was perfect. Exactly what I wanted." She smiled at him.

Liam kissed her once more. "I'll be right back." Liam eased himself off of Emily and walked to the bathroom. When he returned, he carried a warm washcloth. He knelt on the bed behind her and began to help Emily clean up.

"I can do that."

"I know, but I want to. Is that okay?"

Emily nodded, and Liam lay behind her with her back to him. He hitched her leg up over his thigh and wiped her clean with the washcloth. Emily was slightly self-conscious about Liam cleaning her most intimate areas, but remembered that he had already spent a lot of time between her legs. The fact that he wanted to take care of her so…intimately, made her heart skip a beat.

"I told you, I'll always make sure your taken care of," Liam whispered in her ear as if he could hear her thought. He tossed the washcloth on the floor and pulled Emily close. He settled in behind her, pressing his body as close to her as possible, and circled one arm around her waist. His other arm rested under her head.

"Sleep, baby. I'm right here. I've got you. Get some rest because it's still early, and I'm sure I'll wake up in a few hours. And when I do, I'm going to want to make love to you all over again."

Emily sighed and wiggled her butt against him. "Are you still hard?"

"A little bit, yeah."

"Is that normal?" Emily asked in surprise.

"With you," he told her, "I have a feeling it will be. Sleep, baby."

Emily relaxed into him, letting her body melt into the mattress. Liam's warmth and the electrical pulses through her body lulled her into a deep sleep.

***

Rage coursed through him as he watched her make love to another man. The sight before him took him back to the first time he'd caught them together. That time, he had made a mistake. He let his anger overtake his thinking, leading him to destroy his own plans. This time, he'd take her, and she'd have no way of escaping his grasp.

He had no use for the man. His only concern was for her. She was his. He had waited decades, and finally, she would join him. He needed to grow stronger first, to gather enough energy to complete his task, for the curse still worked against him. There was no doubt that she would finally become his, and they would live out their days together in eternity.

Patience was not his strong suit, but he had no choice. The time would come soon enough. He slipped through the walls and drifted down the stairs as an orb of blue, to the place where he could rest, where his power could grow.

Twenty-One

"You stole her!" Banks screamed as he re-entered the room. He'd followed the men who dragged Abigail from the study, and James caught a glimpse of him whispering to them through the crack in the door.

"She doesn't love you," James shouted. His heartbeat erratically, the fear was compounded by his throbbing head. His blurred vision, along with the taste of blood in his mouth, nauseated him. "Let her go! I'm in love with her, and I won't apologize for it. She has the freedom to make her own choices. She doesn't want you!"

Robert Banks' infatuation with Abigail began before she was even old enough to marry.

"You only want—no. You need to keep up your image of the socialite you are, including having a wife to bear your children. When Abigail's father refused your marriage proposal, you took matters into your own hands. Didn't you?"

James watched as Banks paced the room. His boots thumped against the wood floor that sent an eerie echo through the room. Rage filled Banks' eyes. The color gone, replaced by darkness that sent shivers down James' spine.

"You arranged the 'accident' that killed her parents, leaving Abigail *alone?"* Banks stopped pacing. James hoped his theory was wrong, but Banks' change in demeanor proved otherwise. The bile rose in his stomach at the thought that his father's business partner could commit such a crime. *"You thought you could swoop in and take her for your own!"* James screamed at the man who he once considered to be an uncle to him.

"What happened, Banks? Some bad business deals finally catch up to you?"

At his statement, Banks' fist landed across James' already bloody and bruised jaw. Pain coursed through James' head, blurring his vision more.

"You need to take control of her inheritance. You've lost everything, haven't you?"

"Not everything. I'll be taking control of this house soon enough," Banks sneered like a bear prepared to kill its prey. He raised his walking stick in one hand and brought it down, hard, slamming it into the floor. *"She is mine!"* Banks' voice sent vibrations bouncing off the walls in the room. He showed his teeth as he yelled.

"No! She is not! She doesn't belong to you!" James tried to lunge at Banks. His anger growing exponentially with each passing moment. He had never been a violent person, but he was sure he'd strangle Banks with his bare hands if given a chance.

He was halted by the man standing behind him. He pressed on his shoulders, holding him in place. With his hands tied behind him, he had no leverage to use against his captor. James tried to make sense of Banks' last statement. *"You can't take this house. This was my father's house! It's mine!"*

"We'll see about that," Banks said as he pulled a document from the inside pocket of his coat. *"This was a 'business' agreement your father signed on his death bed, making me sole successor to his estate should anything unfortunate happen to you."* Banks paused. *"It was always in my plans to get rid of Henry, and you, and be the sole owner of the*

business. *I just never expected you would seduce her into loving you."*

James' head spun while he knelt on the floor. He bled from the cut on his head, given to him from the beating he'd received after Banks had caught him and Abigail together in his bedroom. Blood dripped down his brow. The faint, muffled cries of Abigail in the background broke his heart more and more as the moments ticked by. He knew Banks was possessive, but he had no idea he was a tyrant. James' mind raced, and all he could think about was Abigail and what Banks' men were doing to her. They had dragged her kicking and screaming from the study, and there was nothing he could do to stop them with his hands being bound behind his back.

The realization that his death was imminent washed over him. There was no doubt about that. Robert Banks would never allow him to live now. He only wished he could see his beautiful Abigail one last time. James' attention was brought back to the present when Banks knelt down in front of him, the document his father had signed in his hand.

"My father would have never signed that."

"Oh no, he wouldn't. Not when he was well. But on his death bed, he could barely speak. He didn't even have the strength to read it, let alone hold the pen. I assisted him. Told him it assured you would have the same control as he did. He was more than happy to let me hold his hand while he scribbled his name."

All hope that James might have had was lost in that instant.

"Charles!" Banks barked. Confusion set in as Banks' own butler entered the room. James looked up and caught Charles' eye. *"Take James' belongings and have them destroyed. He no longer resides in this house,"* Banks instructed.

"Sir?" replied Charles. The confusion was clearly audible in his voice.

"You heard me. I am now the owner of this property. We move in immediately. Have his belongings removed and never mention his

name or Abigail's name again."

James saw the sadness in Charles' eyes as he nodded at Banks' request. Charles turned to look at him. He did his best to plead with him, but there was nothing Charles could do. Not if he wanted to suffer the same fate. And James knew it.

After a moment, Charles gave James the slightest nod. James lowered his eyes and head to the floor as Charles walked out of the room. He was gone, and it was the last time James would ever see the eyes of a kind soul again. As he was dragged to his feet by Banks' men and led down the stairs.

***

Abigail fought as hard as she could, but they were too powerful. She had been hauled down into the basement where she now lay bound and gagged as she watched two men dig. They never mentioned why they were digging, but she somehow knew the hole was for her. Her grave.

Abigail watched as Banks' men beat James. Banks told her she was supposed to be his. Her pleads for him to leave her alone and let her live happily with James went unnoticed. Banks' men tied a gag around her mouth while he paced back and forth in the study like a mad man, saying his plans had been ruined, and she and James would pay. Now she understood what he meant. He hadn't gotten what he wanted—her. So, her punishment would be death, and she knew James would suffer the same fate. The raging beast in Banks was out, and he was going to kill both her and the one man she had ever loved.

The hole was dug, and the two men who worked for Banks picked her up like a rag doll, tossed her down into the pit, and covered her with dirt. She tried to wiggle free, but the binds on her hands and feet wouldn't allow her to move. The ropes cut into her skin. She felt the trickles of blood slick her hands, but she wasn't able to slip them free. Her screams were muffled by the dirty rag tied around her head. Dirt burned and scratched her eyes as she struggled to get free. The musty smell of it sickened her as it seeped into her nose, suffocating her. The weight on top grew with each shovel full of dirt thrown on top of her. Soon, it was too heavy for her to move.

Abigail managed to turn her head to the side and maneuvered the dirt to create a pocket of air around her nose. She opened one eye into a slit and glanced up before the last shovel of loose earth was thrown on to her. Banks stood and smiled down at her. His voice was sinister as he spoke, "We'll be together again."

Abigail was determined to forget his voice. She'd be dammed if it was the last voice she ever heard echoing through her mind as she died. She squeezed her eyes closed and thought of all the happy memories she could of her parents and James. She remembered the sweet words he'd spoken to her. The dreams and plans they had talked about—the promises he made to her until she could no longer think. The lack of air sent her into deep drowsiness.

It was silent, black, and still. She drew in one last labored breath and let herself fall into a heavy sleep with the sound of James' voice distantly calling for her.

***

Liam woke slowly. He tried to open his eyes and force his body to rouse quicker, but the nightmare held him captive. His heart raced, and sweat slicked his skin. The dream had been the same as always. Only this time, he knew the name of the man who hurt him, and it was clear who Abigail was. Emily in another life. Liam couldn't shake the feeling that Robert Banks was the darkness lurking over Emily, hiding like a coward in the basement.

Using all of his strength, Liam rolled toward Emily, freeing his body from the remnants of the nightmare. When he gazed down at her, her cheeks were wet. Silent tears streamed down her skin, her breathing erratic.

"Emily. Baby. Wake up," he shook her shoulders, but she remained unmoving and stuck in her dream.

"Em, come back to me, please. Baby. Wake up!"

The walls swayed, the wood around them creaked, threatening to splinter. The bed rolled side to side. Rumbling resounded through the walls. Liam tucked Emily underneath him and hoped the quake didn't last too long. Emily whimpered, and he knew she was fighting to wake up. Her eyelids opened into slits, and her beautiful warm brown eyes hit him.

"James?" Emily asked.

"Wake up, baby," Liam said again. The shaking strengthened. The sounds of the walls moving intensified, sending a vibrating roar through the flat. A sound that Liam couldn't remember experiencing in the past.

"What's happening?" Emily's eyes were wide as she fought to find her bearings in the chaos of the moment.

"Earthquake," Liam confirmed. "It's stopping now. Don't worry. I want you to wake up in case there is a bigger one. You had another nightmare, didn't you?"

"Liam!" Emily shouted. Becoming aware, "Liam! You're James! I remember!"

Liam kissed and hug her tight. "Shhhh. I know. And you're Abigail."

At his confirmation, Emily broke down. "Liam, he buried me. Alive. He found us together, and he buried me."

"What!" Liam's heart sank. He knew Banks had done something unthinkable to them both, but knowing that Emily now had memories of being buried alive broke him. "It's okay. It's okay," Liam soothed.

"It's not okay. He's still here! He told me before they finish throwing dirt on me that me and him would be together again. He's going to try and kill me again and keep me captive in this house. The spirit is him!"

At Emily's horrifying statement, the door that had been open to the bedroom slammed with so much force, the photos on Liam's dresser were knocked over. Not even the earthquake that had just passed under them had enough energy to move them. Liam knew it was Banks, and the knowledge that the son of a bitch was in his bedroom, hiding, invisibly, made his blood boil. Now that he remembered what Banks had done to him and Emily in a past life, he was readying for war. Banks lied to Abigail; he'd lied to everyone. He murdered Abigail's parents, leaving her an orphan with no one to care for her at that time, to try and force her to marry him, and lied to James' father. He murdered Abigail because she refused his hand in marriage. He'd been planning on killing James all along to take over the business. Now, the jealous prick was still trying to control Emily from his grave.

Liam bolted out of bed and bellowed, "Banks! You're done here. Leave! You're dead, and we are alive. You're not tearing us apart again. We know who you are and what you did. Go to hell and leave us alone. You murdered us. This is *your* punishment. Seeing us alive and happy together!"

"Liam," Emily whispered. Liam's chest heaved, and he shook with rage. He watched as Emily crawled across the bed to where he stood. She reached for him, wrapping her arms around his waist. She nuzzled into his chest and held him tightly until his breathing slowed. "He's gone. For now. I don't feel him here anymore."

"Yes, I think you're right. Are you okay?" Liam asked while looking down at her. She was trembling.

"Come back to bed?"

"Yes."

Climbing back into bed, he pulled Emily tight against him. "I'm so sorry." Liam's voice hitched as he spoke.

"It's okay," Emily soothed. She touched his shoulder and stroked his skin. "We'll fight him. He won't win. We won't let that happen. We're together now, and he can't tear us apart."

Liam buried his face in her hair, inhaling her warm vanilla scent. He found it calmed his nerves, and his breathing slowed. "You're right. That's exactly what we are going to do. Fight."

Emily inhaled and relaxed against him. She wiggled her ass against his hardening erection. He couldn't help his body's response with her nakedness pressed against him. The dark sheets bunched around her waist, highlighting her pale skin.

"Is it weird that I'm having erotic thoughts after what had just happened?" Emily asked. Liam smiled into the back of her neck.

"How are you feeling this morning?" he asked her. As promised, Liam had woken up a few hours after they'd fallen asleep the first time and made love to Emily again. And again, a third time a few hours later.

"Mmm. I feel good."

"You sure? Not too sore?"

"I'm deliciously sore," Emily admitted. She smiled and craned her neck back to look at Liam.

"Deliciously sore? Oh, baby. Come here."

Liam rolled to his back, taking Emily and settling her on top of him. She straddled his hips when he noticed she was still trembling. Wrapping his hand to the back of her neck, he pulled her down close, so they were nose to nose. "Look at me, Emily. Fuck him. He isn't going to win this time. You and me, we're going to be together whether he likes it or not. Nothing is keeping us apart from now on. You came back here, to this city and to this house for a reason. I believe everything happens for a reason, and me moving into this place and you coming back here is because now is the time for us to finally be together. Nothing will stand in our way. This is our reward for going through that atrocity."

Emily nodded. "You're right. I don't know all of the details, but I know I didn't want him. I detested him."

Liam pulled her closer. "He can't hurt you anymore. I won't let him. Neither will Trey or Luke. We'll get rid of him. I promise."

Emily lowered her lips so that they gently brushed Liam's. "I know we will. Together, we'll get rid of him."

Liam took her mouth and kissed her until she was breathless.

"Make love to me, Liam."

"Are you sure? You're deliciously sore already. I don't want to hurt you anymore."

Emily didn't respond with words. Instead, she pulled her knees up so they were at Liam's torso and started to lower herself onto his length. Liam wanted to stop her, to make her take a bath and relax before they made love again, but he couldn't bring himself to say the words. Emily knew what she wanted when she wanted it and pursued her desires. She had no qualms with asking for more or telling Liam what she needed throughout their night of lovemaking. So, he let her take the lead, knowing she'd stop and tell him if she was too uncomfortable.

He helped guide himself into her as she lowered herself.

Liam watched as Emily threw her head back. Her brown waves hung around her back and shoulders, almost touching her hips, as she savored the feel of him inside of her and exhaling her pleasure. She started to lift herself, but Liam stopped her. "Rock back and forth, baby. It'll be easier on you that way. Just grind yourself on me."

And she did. All the while, Liam kept his hands on her hips, helping her move against him. It took everything in him not to thrust himself up and pump into her, but he wasn't about to take her hard, yet.

"Baby, touch yourself. Make yourself come. I can't hold on much longer."

Emily reached down and began to rub her swollen clit. "That's it," Liam groaned. He moved his hands to Emily's firm breasts. They filled his hands, and he gently squeezed while flicking her nipples. The movement of her hips increased, sending waves of pleasure through his body. Liam sat up and wrapped his arms around Emily's back. He hugged her tight, pressing her nakedness into his own hot, electrified skin. "Let go, Em. Don't think about anything but us. Nothing else matters right now. Just you and me. And this."

Emily threw her head back. Liam lowered his mouth to her neck and nibbled at the sensitive flesh.

"Liam," she gasped, and he felt her tremble and whimper in his arms from pleasure. Moments later, Liam groaned his own release into her neck. His body spent and sated, he laid back on the bed, bringing Emily with him. She rested on top of his body, her head nuzzled in his own neck. Liam caressed her back when a thought came to him. "Em?"

"Humm?"

His hand found her head, where he threaded his fingers through the thick strands. "We didn't use a condom that time."

"It's okay. I'm on the pill."

"You are?"

Emily lifted her head. Her eyes were still heavy from their lovemaking. A rosy glow painted her cheeks. "Yeah. I went on it a couple years ago. I wanted to be prepared. Just in case I met the right person," she said as she kissed him.

"I haven't been with anyone in over a year," Liam stated. "And I've never not used a condom."

"I trust you, honey."

Liam rolled and shifted them to their sides. They lay together like that for a long time, sleeping on and off before Liam got up and drew a bath for both of them.

Twenty-Two

Liam cooked them both some breakfast and called Trey and Luke. He filled them in on the latest dream that he and Emily had, and his teammates were now working on finding evidence that could explain their dreams. He also told them about the incident with the slamming door early that morning. His friends informed him that there were no earthquakes reported that day and neither of them felt anything. That left Liam with a sick feeling in the pit of his stomach. Just how dangerous was the spirit of Banks if he were able to shake an entire house? It was something he really didn't want to think about at the moment, but also couldn't seem to keep his mind from going back to that question.

"Liam?"

"Yeah?"

"Are you okay? You seem distracted."

Emily was curled up into his side on the couch while they watched a movie. Liam hugged her tight and snuggled deeper into the sofa cushions with her at his side. "Yeah. I'm good. Just thinking a lot."

"Tell me?"

"I was just thinking," he said as he kissed her head, "how did you like running the cameras that night when you investigated with us?"

Liam considered telling her that his thoughts were more on the subject of Banks but decided he would hold off on sharing his concerns. His theory that Banks' infatuation with Emily was the reason for his staying behind and following her plagued him. He had dealt with hostile spirits in the past, entities that refused to move on due to fear or a desire to control the living. But he never imagined he'd learn that the spirit haunting his building murdered him in another life. And, it was still after his love. She'd been taken from him once before. He'd be damned if the son of a bitch tried to harm her again. He was a paranormal investigator. He lived for chasing ghosts. Thrived on walking into places swarming with paranormal activity. He just didn't know how to keep Emily safe from a dead man who wanted her all to himself. How do you protect someone from an unseen force?

Their morning had already been disrupted, and he was going to do everything he possibly could to keep their days and nights relaxed and peaceful.

"I enjoyed it. I was actually going to ask if I could investigate with you again. I want to learn more about paranormal work."

"Seriously? You were?"

"Yeah. Why?"

"I didn't think you'd want to continue investigating after what happened. But I'm happy to hear you've been thinking about it. How do you feel about managing the office once we get it up and running? I already talked to the guys about it. They're on board if you are. We think you'd be a great team member. But only if you really want. I don't want you to give up your photography business if that's what you really want to do. You can investigate with us if you want when we have a local location. And travel with us if you want as much as you want."

"I'd love to. You really want me to work with you guys?"

"Yes. I want you to work with me. With us. With my team. I want you by my side as much as possible. I feel grounded when you're near me. I know that makes me sound like a selfish, obsessive prick, but baby, it's the truth. I had no idea how lonely and miserable I was until you came into my life. When I'm near you, I'm a better person."

Emily kissed him. "Yes. I would love to work with you. To be honest, I've been thinking about changing things up. I love photography, and I'm not ready to give it up completely yet, but I think I need a change of pace. I'd love to come along and travel with you guys when it's not wedding season. I don't know how much I'll want to be inside of the locations. I definitely don't want to be alone in any room by myself. At least not yet. But maybe I can keep watch in the van. Let you guys know if I see anything out of the ordinary on the cameras. Maybe I can help you guys go over footage too. Lately, I've been feeling like something is missing. Now I know what."

"What?" Liam asked. Emily scooted up and brought her face closer to his. Her warm, brown eyes hit him, and the flames in his belly grew.

"After you told me about your childhood home and what your family went through, I decided I want to help people. I don't want anyone to feel helpless the way you guys did, or the way I have. If I can help someone figure out the truth, then that's what I want to do. I would love to help you guys run things."

Liam smiled from ear to ear. "The guys are going to be happy. I'm excited and relieved."

Emily looked at him, confused. "Relieved?"

"Uh-huh. Now I don't have to leave you as much when we have to investigate out of town. You'll be coming with us."

"That sounds wonderful. So amazing and exciting, Liam!" Emily's voice carried an enthusiasm he hadn't yet heard. Her eyes were bright with wonder as thoughts fluttered through her mind. "I've never traveled before. I always stayed around Seattle before moving here. I want to travel and see the country. Maybe the world too."

"There's so much to see, and I can't wait to share it with you. But first, I talked to the guys this morning. We decided we need to make us a priority right now. We put off booking any more investigations for the next couple of weeks. We are going to get to the bottom of what is going on in this house."

"Are you sure you can put off investigations? I don't want it to hurt your business."

"Yeah. It will be okay. Unless something comes up that might be an emergency, we won't book for the next couple of weeks. Plus, if I'm going to turn this place into headquarters, we need to figure out what's going on."

"That is true. What can I do to help?"

"Keep being cute," he told her in a sexy tone. She laughed, and he pulled her closer. So close, he was afraid he would crush her. But he couldn't help the desire within him to feel her pressed against his body. "Seriously, Em," Liam continued, "just keep being yourself. The best thing we can do is not let that fucker know he's affecting us. Keep being happy, laugh, enjoy life and each other. I'm not going to let it win, Em. You don't belong to him. You never did."

A cold breeze washed over them while Liam stared into Emily's eyes. Seconds later, a low rumble, similar to the one they heard hours earlier, resounded in the walls, and the door to the bathroom slammed shut. Emily's eyes widened with fear. Liam squeezed her tight and turned her head back toward him, holding her eyes with his. "He won't win," he told her sternly. "We will get rid of him."

"I know. I believe you. I'm so much stronger with you. We'll fight him and show him that he can't hurt us anymore. I'm yours, Liam."

Without thinking, Liam stood and took her hand, pulling her up with him, and he led her to the bedroom. He moved quickly and with purpose. "Liam. What are you doing?" Emily asked him.

"I'm sick and tired of this asshole thinking he has control over you. Over us. So, I'm going to show him again who you really belong to. And it's not him."

"What if we piss him off? What if he turns more violent?"

"His days are numbered, baby. The guys are coming over tomorrow. Trey texted me a little while ago. He has some info he wants to share with us. And he might have a plan on how we can get rid of Banks."

Twenty-Three

"Damn. You look like shit," Luke said as he climbed the stairs to Liam's house.

"Thanks, asshole," Liam told his friend before pulling him in for a manly hug.

"Seriously, man. What's wrong? You look terrible." Trey came up behind Luke.

Liam held out his hand and excepted the coffee cup that Trey gave him. "I haven't slept much," Liam told his teammates, taking a sip of coffee.

"Anything else happen after we talked yesterday?" Trey asked.

"Feeling like we're being watched, constantly," Liam confirmed. "Cold breezes. The rumbling in the walls has become more frequent. Em's nightmares have gotten worse, and she's having multiple dreams a night now. So am I. I stay awake as long as possible, so I can wake her up when she's having a nightmare."

Liam took a seat on one of the steps. "Before we go in, Trey, fill me in on what's going on. What did you find? I need to know so I can be there for Em as much as possible and not be shocked when I hear. She's scared to hear what you found out. I wanna give her some time alone before we go in."

"Alright. This took a lot of digging. I was able to trace Phil to a distant relative. A great, great, great grandfather, named Charles Randall. He used to live in this house. He was a butler here. But here's the kicker." Trey placed one foot on a step in front of him and leaned in. "Remember we learned about Robert Banks in that news article when we were in Carmel?"

Liam felt his face pale at Trey's mention of Banks' name but nodded to let Trey know to continue.

"Charles was Banks' butler and his cousin back in the mid-eighteen hundreds. They both lived in this house."

"Phil's last name was Randall. So, it's very possible that they were distant relatives," Liam stated. His head spun from the new information he'd received. Phill had been distantly related to a man who killed him and Emily.

"Yeah. I'm still doing some digging with that. It's a popular surname, so it's going to take some time for me to sort that out. But that's not what interested me the most."

"What did interest you?" Liam asked hesitantly. Not sure he could take any more news.

Trey reached around and pulled a file from his bag. Liam took the file and opened it. He was instantly frozen with shock. He couldn't believe what he was looking at. An old printed photo of himself standing next to a man who he knew as Robert Banks. A man who he had only met in his dreams.

The men in the photo had their arms around each other, each with a cigar in their hand, and they were smiling. Liam was speechless. He flipped the paper over, revealing another photo, one of Emily standing with an older gentleman and an older woman, whom he assumed was Abigail's parents. They were dressed in party attire, standing outside of the house he and Emily now resided in. Before he could utter a word, Trey said, "Her name was—"

"Abigail," Liam interjected, finishing his sentence. "Emily was Abigail."

"Holy Shit!" Luke muttered, "So she's Abigail from the EVP we caught?"

The bile in Liam's stomach churned. The validation of Trey's research confirming his suspicions overtook him. Without warning, he stood, leaned over the railing, and heaved into some bushes below, emptying the contents of his stomach.

When Liam was finished, he sat back down just as Luke walked back over from his truck, carrying a bottle of water. He handed it to Liam. "Thanks."

"What's going on, brother?" Trey asked.

Liam dropped his head. "I don't know. This is a lot. We knew what we were dealing with, but this," he held up the file to his friends, "this confirms it. It's surreal." Blowing out a breath, he took a sip of the water and let his head hang down again.

"What else, man? We've never seen you like this. Talk to us," Luke said while taking a seat next to Liam.

Trey moved in closer, leaning against the railing.

Liam turned his head toward Luke. "I love her."

"Yeah. We know."

"I'm scared of losing her again. I couldn't protect her then. What if I can't protect her now?"

"You didn't have us then. You have us now," Trey stated. "You're family. That means Emily is family. We won't let anything happen to her or to you. Have you told her? That you love her?"

"Not yet."

"You should. Because she feels the same."

Liam looked at Luke again. He squinted his eyes as he asked, "How do you know?"

"I see the way you two look at each other. You practically undress each other with your stares. She's only got eyes for you, man. Look. I don't know much about falling in love and shit. It's never happened to me. But if it does, I want my girl to look at me the way Emily looks at you."

"So much has happened these last few weeks. We found out we were lovers in another life. That we were murdered by a man who now haunts this house. Emily's been tormented by him her entire life."

"So, tell her," Luke reiterated. "I'm telling you. She loves you right back."

"You really think so?"

"Yeah! I really think so. The woman's practically got fuckin' heart emojis coming out of her eyes when she looks at you."

All three friends bellowed in laughter for what seemed like several minutes. Leave it to Luke to always find a way to lighten a mood. After they were able to pull themselves together, Liam asked, "Were you able to find out anything about her parents?"

Trey shook his head. "No, I'm still trying. But it's like she told us. She was abandoned. Left at a fire station. Her mother never stated who she was. I think that's a dead-end for us." Trey paused, giving Liam a moment. "From what I can gather, the two men in the first picture are Robert Banks and James Watson. James worked for Robert."

"Yeah, I know. He was a bookkeeper. His father was a business partner of Banks. James started working for him after his father died. I remember all of it from my dreams. There are more details now."

Trey continued, "The man behind them is this man here…" Trey pulled another copy of a photo from the back of the stack of papers. "This is Charles. One of Phil's great grandfathers."

Liam stared at the photo. The man bared a striking resemblance to Phil. He felt the stares of his teammates on him when Trey spoke, "You think this dark entity is Banks, don't you."

"I'm willing to bet everything I own that it's him."

Trey ran his hands down his face. When he looked up, he noticed a woman approaching from across the street. "You expecting anyone?" he asked Liam.

"No. Why?"

The sound of the gate at the bottom of the stairs caught Liam's attention, and he looked up. A short woman, shorter than Emily, with a dark brunette pixie haircut approached them. She eyed the three men before walking, continuing her strides up the steps. Her eyes fixed on Liam.

"You must be Liam Wesley," she stated, very confidently. "I recognize you from the photo Em sent me."

Liam smiled, closed the folder, and handed it to Trey as he headed down the steps. "Lexi."

Twenty-Four

Emily stared at the photos laid out on the coffee table in front of her. Both Lexi and Liam sat on either side of her on the sofa, acting as anchors to the raging oceans of information and emotions swirling around her. The photos before her confirming the dreams of a past life with Liam, sent shock waves through her.

Emily was overtaken with emotion when Liam called her downstairs, and Lexi stood waiting for her. Having her best friend with her, along with Liam, at that moment was definitely keeping her calm. When Lexi and the guys came into her flat, Liam shared that Trey had more information for them but insisted she eat, have some coffee, and visit with Lexi a bit. Now, everyone was gathered in her living room. The space felt cramped, but she was thankful for the company. The prickling sensation of Banks' presence had her on edge. Emily wasn't a person who carried animosity in her heart, but the amount of hate and revulsion she felt toward Banks bubbled to the surface.

"I'm sorry, Emily. I'm still trying to figure out who your birth mother was," Trey assured.

"I know. It's okay. Like I said, I've made peace with it. I appreciate you trying."

"So, this Charles. He was a distant grandfather of your now

deceased landlord?" Lexi asked while gesturing with her arms in the air. Lexi was notorious for talking with her hands. She was small, but she made a big statement with her presence.

"Yes," Liam confirmed.

"And he left this building to you? So now you own all of this? The same house where Robert Banks and James lived?"

Liam nodded at Lexi's statement.

"Wow," she stated as she picked her coffee mug off the table. The multiple rings on her fingers, clinking the porcelain.

"Yeah. Wow," Emily agreed with her friend. "So, now what? We have this information. What do we do now?"

Liam broke the silence in the room. "Somethings bugging me."

"What is it?" Emily asked, placing her hand on his shoulder. He'd picked the photo of Banks up off of the table and stared at it.

"I don't know. We're still missing a piece to the puzzle. Why would Banks hang back after he died? It's almost like he's been waiting for you." Liam's eyes hit Emily. His intense blues warmed her entire body. His hand came up and brushed her cheek before wrapping around, where he gently massaged her neck. "He's haunted you all these years, and then one day you felt the urge to move here. You showed up, and he became more violent. There's something else. I think we need to dig."

Trey and Luke stared at Liam in confusion. "Dig?" They both asked in unison.

Liam looked at Emily again. "Em, you said your dreams were becoming clearer. You saw Banks' men digging a hole in the basement. They threw you into it?" Emily nodded in confirmation.

"So, yes. I say we dig. I'm not saying we will find anything. But we need to try to find some kind of evidence. What if Abigail's body was never found? What if she's still buried here. Maybe we'll find clues that *someone* was buried under this house at one time. Maybe we'll find something else entirely. This is an old fucking house. Passed down from generation to generation in Phil's family. One of his grandfathers was a butler for Banks. We know that Banks not only had Abigail's parents killed but also James and Abigail as well. We also know he tricked James' dying father into signing over this house to him. The minute Em showed up, and I went to the basement, the energy in this house flipped. Like it knew we were together again. So yeah, I say let's dig. Let's tear up the ground down there and see what we find. Maybe we'll piss it off, but I don't care. The truth has been hidden for far too long. It's time everything comes out."

"I'm staying to help," Lexi stated, matter of factly. "Before you start with me, Em, I've already made up my mind. You've been living with this bullshit for far too long. You've found happiness with Liam. I'll be damned if I sit back and watch this thing try to rip it away from you again. So, I'm staying here, and I'm going to help in any way I can."

"But what about your job and your sister?" Emily asked.

"I gave my notice. I have an interview next week at a resort in Napa." Lexi waved her hand nonchalantly in the air as she sat back on the sofa. She angled her body slightly and crossed her legs. "Em, you know I've wanted a change. It's okay. I have money put away. I've already had a few over the phone interviews too. They just want to meet me and have me see the property before I commit to the position. And Tessa wants to move down this way to finish up school."

"You're moving here?" Emily asked with excitement and tears in her eyes.

"Yes!"

***

The women hugged again and cried happy tears while they chatted about the logistics of Lexi's move to the Bay Area. Liam turned to his friends, but before he could say anything, Luke answered for him. "Trey and I will go to the hardware store and grab the equipment we may need. When we get back, we'll start right away."

Liam walked his friends to the front door. "Make sure to grab something to bust that lock downstairs."

"Will do," Trey said.

"Hey, Luke. You're cousin still an engineer for the city?"

Luke turned and caught Liam's eye. He nodded. "Yeah, he is. Why?"

"I need someone to come look at the house. I want to do a lot of renovating. I need to know what I need to do to accomplish it."

"What kind of renovating you looking to do?" Trey stopped and turned to face Luke and Liam.

"For starters, I want to make this our headquarters."

"No shit? Really?" Both men seemed excited at the idea.

Liam continued, "Yes. And I want to expand the upstairs. Emily and I have talked, and she's moving in with me."

Trey and Luke congratulated their friend on his statement. "Happy for you, man," Luke said.

"Thanks. How do you guys really feel about her?"

"Dude, she's awesome. Really. Why?" Trey asked.

"She wants to come on board, help us manage the office. She even wants to travel to locations with us when she has downtime with her photography business. She said she needs a change. She wants to help people. Wants to travel. She's serious and wants to learn more about doing paranormal investigations and help us."

"Tell her we are stoked to have her on board," Trey said.

As they walked out of the building, Luke turned to Liam. "I'll contact my cousin. Ask him to help or maybe recommend someone. This place is gonna be awesome. Let's clean house so we can get started."

A few hours later, after Luke and Trey had returned with a couple of sledgehammers, shovels, and a wheelbarrow, and got started right away with setting up all of their equipment. Knowing that it would take them at least half a day to break up the concrete slab in the basement, Liam, Trey, and Luke decided it would be best to get into the locked apartment and work on digging the next day. Gathering as much evidence as possible was a top priority for everyone. Luke was in the van parked in front, checking the monitors and ensuring all of the cameras were positioned at the right angles. Trey and Lexi were in Liam's apartment, setting up some cameras while Liam and Emily were in her flat setting up.

Liam had finished setting up a few cameras in the back of the apartment when he walked into the living room. Emily was taping down cords that were running from cameras that she had just set up. She hadn't noticed him watching her.

"How are you doing, baby?"

Emily jumped. "Oh my god!" she yelled, her hands pressed to her heart, "You scared me."

Liam hurried to her and pulled her up and embraced her. "I'm sorry. Are you okay?"

"Yes. I'm okay. I feel a little on edge. Obviously, a little jumpy. But I'm okay."

"If things get really intense, I want you to leave the building and go sit in the van. I don't want anything to happen to you. You're new at this and have a lot to learn still."

"I want to be here. I need to be here."

"I know you do. You know we will share everything with you. Being in the van still makes you a hundred percent a part of this team. Like I said, there is still so much for you to learn. Whatever this thing is seems to be hell-bent on destroying us. You've gotten this far without being physically harmed by it, and I want to keep it that way. Lexi already told Trey that she doesn't mind being in the van and keeping an eye on all the cameras. If things get intense, you'll be with her. You'll be able to keep an eye on us from the van. Just like last time. Okay?"

"Guys?" Luke called from the outside hallway. Liam and Emily made their way to the front door and looked around the corner. Trey looked down from the top landing.

"Yeah?" Both Liam and Trey said in unison.

"I'm getting ready to break this lock," Luke called from the end of the hall.

Liam glanced at Emily. She gave him a subtle nod. He took her hand and walked toward Luke. Lexi followed Trey down the stairs from the upper level of the building. "We're right behind you."

Twenty-Five

Trey and Luke stood on either side of Liam while Emily and Lexi hung back. He held a pair of bolt clippers in his hand, with the cutting end around the shackle of the large, heavy-duty lock. It took a bit of muscle, but the cutters broke through the steel, and the lock fell to the basement floor with a loud clunk. Trey took the tool and rested it to the side, against the wall. Liam reached for Emily's hand, and with his other, he turned the doorknob, revealing the mysterious room.

A lone lightbulb with a string hung a few feet past the threshold. Liam stumbled as he stepped to it. "Be careful," he told everyone. "There's a small drop." He pulled the thin string, and the room was basked in an eerie, dim light. The sight before him was unexpected. The room wasn't an apartment as he initially believed. It was a barren room filled with boxes, dozens of them stacked to one side. It was cold and more like a cellar with cinderblock walls. Aside from the boxes stacked to the side, the room was empty.

The concrete slab of the basement stopped a few inches past the doorway, and that was what caused Liam to trip as he entered. They were now standing on a dirt floor, the building's original foundation, with the boxes sitting on wooden pallets.

"I thought this was an apartment," Emily said from beside Liam.

"So did I," he admitted.

"What is all of this stuff?" Lexi asked. She waved her hands around and turned in a circle, taking in all of the room.

Trey pulled a box off of a wood pallet in the center of the room and opened it. On it sat a bouquet of dried, purple flowers that looked like they had been left recently. And a sealed white envelope.

"Trey, can I see those flowers?" Emily asked, pointing to the bouquet. Trey handed them to her. Emily turned to Liam.

"What is it, baby?"

"When we were at your parent's house, your mom said I reminded her of an Anemone."

"A windflower," Liam clarified. "These are windflowers."

"They are. I looked them up when we got back home. I recognized them."

"Windflowers, particularly ones that are purple, are traditionally given to people for protection against evil spirits," Luke announced. "I remember reading it a long time ago in some book about symbolism."

Liam grazed the wilted petals with his fingertips. "Before we left for that last investigation out of town, before you moved in Emily, Phil sent me a message saying he would stop by to grab something from here. I completely forgot about that. He must have left these."

"Do you think he knew who you two were?" Luke asked.

"I don't know for sure. But my gut is saying yes," Liam answered. "Now that I think about it. The last time I talked to him on the phone, he sounded thrilled. I'd never heard him sound that happy before. He was so glad you were moving in, Emily."

Liam pulled the lid off of the box that the flowers had sat on and started looking through the papers inside. "Phil placed the bouquet and that envelope on this box. He wanted us to find this and open it first." Trey and Luke joined him in looking through the box.

Trey handed the sealed envelope to Liam. It was addressed to both him and Emily.

"What does it say?" Emily asked.

Liam read it out loud.

Liam and Emily,

If you're reading this, then I am most likely dead. Don't be sad. It was my time. I've lived long enough and held on to all of these secrets for as long as I could. It's time the truth finally be known.

I was given the responsibility of guarding this house and its secrets when my father died. The seer who my father met with after Banks' death came to me as a young boy and placed a spell upon me. One that would keep me alive. I was to live for as long as it took until the two of you found each other. Until the strings of the universe that each of you holds came together and bound with one another again. The moment I met you, Liam, I knew who you were. I, like my father before me, have guarded this secret for a long time. When Emily contacted me about the apartment, I saw her picture, and I knew that Abigail was coming home.

Everyone gasped. Emily clasped her hands to her mouth, tears welled in her eyes. Liam pulled her close, and Lexi went to her other side, comforting her friend. Liam handed the handwritten letter to Trey, and he continued.

Liam, I'm sure in your line of work you have developed some good instincts. Trust them. They will keep you safe and continue to lead you to the truth. Emily, I never formally met you in this life, but I want you to know that Liam and his friends can and should be trusted. They won't let any harm come to you. I've lived my life haunted by the dark spirit, and I assume he has been haunting you two as well in some way. He is dark, and he is evil. Trust your instincts and end him.

My father started a journal of what he witnessed and kept documentation of everything. I've continued to collect and keep documents over the years in hopes that one day they would help in any way. That's why this room has always been sealed off. These walls have held the secrets for over a century. They have confined the evil in this house to this one room.

Read the journals, take them, and use them. End this and finally live together as you should have been able to do before. I'm only sorry that I can't be with you to see it.

Good Luck
-Phillip Randall

"Holy shit!" Luke said while running his hand over his face. "Phillip is Charles' son! Not his great-grandson!"

"My God," Liam stated.

Everyone stood stock-still. Liam looked down at Emily, her face wet from tears. "It's okay, baby."

"I can't believe this. I mean, I do believe it. It's happening. But knowing that someone I never even had a chance to meet knew all along what happened and what would happen is...surreal."

Lexi walked over to the box and picked up a book from inside. "It's a journal. It looks like it belonged to Charles."

Trey knelt next to her. "Sure is. There's a lot here, Liam. It could take days to go through all of this stuff. What do you want to do?"

Liam thought for a minute, then looked at his two best friends. "I'd like to go through all of this. But, the reality is we already have a lot of information, and Em and I can't live like this anymore. We want to move on with our lives. We can't do that with some asshole spirit lurking over us. Lexi, how do you feel about combing through some of this stuff while we get started?"

"Absolutely. I'll help in any way I can. Em, you want to help me?"

"Yes, of course."

"We are ending this now." Liam looked at his friends as he spoke. "But we are going to need help,"

Twenty-Six

"I'm calling Dave. If anyone can help us, it's him." Trey told everyone while pulling his phone out of his back pocket.

"Who's Dave?" Emily asked as she turned to Liam.

"He's a friend of ours. He's a psychic medium. Sometimes, we call him when we have a tough case and need help communicating with spirits, especially with poltergeists. He's helped us with a lot of cases in the past. We trust him, and he is always willing to help us."

"Poltergeists? That's a real thing?" Lexi asked. But before anyone could answer, she continued, "I'm sorry. I don't mean to sound dumb. I thought Poltergeist was only a movie."

"The term was popularized by the movie," Trey answered. "But a poltergeist haunting is very much a real thing. It's the German word for noisy ghost. It's when a spirit is able to move objects, even people. It's an intelligent spirit that can make loud noises by moving objects or banging on walls. That's not a dumb question at all," Trey stated. "Most people don't know or understand the different types of hauntings, and that's how misconceptions are started."

"Thank you." Lexi nodded at Trey before looking back down into the open box. "Always feel free to ask us if you have a question.

We're happy to answer them."

"I will," Lexi stated while tucking a lock of hair behind her ear.

"We should keep setting up. Trey, let us know what Dave says."

"I will." Trey pushed the button on his phone to call the psychic medium. Luke cleared an area where they wanted to dig. Liam carried the box they had discovered and opened, while he, Emily, and Lexi moved back upstairs to finish setting up camera equipment.

Hours later, Emily and Lexi were reading through the documents when Emily called out to Liam. "You should take a look at this page." She handed the open journal that Charles kept to Liam.

Liam read the journal entry and stared at the page in disbelief. "This was written by Charles. He explains what happened to Banks and how he inherited the property." Liam paused and strode to the front door. "Guys," he shouted for his teammates. Moments later, Trey and Luke entered Emily's flat.

Liam stood in the middle of the room and read the journal entry.

April 25, 1870
I buried Robert today. The sickness finally took over his body. Despite the sadness of the situation, I feel nothing but relief. The sun shone brightly at the cemetery. The house has never felt as warm as it does.

May 1, 1870
The spirit, of whom I am sure is Robert, has been haunting the house. I feel he's angry at my inheritance of the property. Though, he should be angry at himself since he never named another next of kin in his will. I've sent for a seer woman to come and help me communicate with him. Rumor is she is a powerful witch. I feel my family is in danger now. I received word today that Robert's closest men died in a tragic accident. No one knows how. It seems they dropped dead for no reason. They were the only ones, besides myself who knew what Robert had

done.

May 3, 1870
My wife and I were both dragged out of our beds last night by unseen hands. Little Phillip has been seeing a "Shadow Man."

"Oh my god," Emily said, pressing her hands to her mouth.
"I bet Banks was the cause of his men's deaths," Trey said.
"Trying to hide his secrets, even from the grave," Luke added.
"There's more," Liam continued reading.

May 10, 1870
They seer visited last night. She saw everything that Banks had done. The walls of the house vibrated and rumbled as she spoke, revealing his sins. She was unable to remove him from the home. Apparently, he refused to move on and believes he can continue ruling with an iron fist from the grave. She placed a spell on him, binding him to the confines of the house.
While she looked into her crystal ball, the future showed itself to her. Her vision showed that James and Abigail will return one day. Until that time, my family and I have been tasked with guarding this house, ensuring that the truth is revealed when the time comes.

May 13, 1870
I had James and Emily's bodies moved to the cemetery today, and the room they were buried in sealed shut. The house has remained quiet since the seer visited. I only hope it stays that way. I have no intention of breaking my promise. I'll remain here and do whatever is necessary to make sure James and Abigail can return to this place and learn the truth."

"That's the end of this journal," Liam said as he closed it and sat on Emily's sofa. She took a seat next to him, her arm around his shoulders.

Trey spoke, "Liam, if Charles moved the bodies, we might not be able to find them."

"Why's that?" Emily asked. Her brown drawn together in question.

"Because in the early nineteen hundreds, San Francisco passed a law, prohibiting any further burials in the city. And in 1914, it passed another law that any bodies in cemeteries within the city limits needed to be relocated. They were all moved to Colma, just south of here. That's why there are so many cemeteries there. It was meant to be a Necropolis. Any bodies who weren't claimed in cemeteries in San Francisco were buried in mass graves in Colma. And the old cemeteries in the city were destroyed for housing development."

Liam sat, holding the journal while he listened to Trey speak. "Right. So, unless Charles paid to have the bodies moved, they would have been relocated to a mass, unmarked grave. Can we try to find out?"

"It would be nice to know if they were buried properly a third time." Emily looked from Liam to Trey as she spoke.

"I'll do everything I can to try and find out where they are," Trey assured.

"Alright. Let's keep going. Lexi, thanks. This information is really helpful. You have no idea. We're not stopping now. We keep going and dig anyway. Just to be sure they aren't still here." Liam turned his attention to Trey. "Did you get a hold of Dave?"

"Yep," Trey answered. "He promised he'd be here later tonight."

"Perfect," Liam said as he rose from the sofa. Trey and Luke went back to setting up equipment throughout the house.

A few hours later, Emily and Lexi were in the kitchen making coffee while the guys were in the living room going over the plan for the night.

Emily walked into the living room, carrying a tray. Lexi followed close behind with a tray of cream and sugar. Liam caught the movement of Lexi, jerking forward as if she were being pushed from behind. Her back arched, and her arms flew out in front of her to catch herself as she hit the floor. The tray she was carrying crashed to the floor and was knocked to the side. Emily was next to be pushed and knocked down, spilling the hot coffee everywhere.

The guys were up and moving toward them as soon as they realized what had happened. The lights flickered, and there was a low rumbling sound coming from within the walls again. Static swirled around. The air was charged with energy.

"What happened?" Trey asked once he reached Lexi.

"There was a cold breeze that rushed up behind me and pushed me. Seriously, pushed me! I felt hands on my back, but I know no one was behind me. It knocked me down. Then Emily went down, and everything in here went nuts!" Lexi shouted.

Liam held Emily tight against him. Trey doing the same with Lexi. Luke moved the dropped trays out of the way so no one would trip on them.

Emily threw her hands up in the air and screamed. "Fuck! That was my favorite mug, you asshole! Why don't you just leave! You're pitiful." She was yelling at the air, spinning around, searching for the unseen entity. Everyone's eyes had gone wide in surprise. Liam had never seen Emily upset. Not that they had known each other for a particularly long time, but he knew this was way out of the ordinary for her. "You keep your filthy hands off my friend. Why do you keep hiding? Why don't you show—"

"Em, stop." Liam grabbed hold of her shoulders. "Don't antagonize him right now."

"I hate him, Liam. I hate him so much. I want to kill him."

"Baby, when did you get this?" Liam traced his finger down her arm. Three scratch marks were visible, and he watched as they turned to welts.

Emily shook her head. "I don't know. They weren't there when I was in the kitchen. Did I bump my arm on something when I fell?"

Luke came up with his phone and took a picture. "We've seen this before."

"Yeah." Liam smoothed his hand over her arm. "Spirits will scratch to try and get a point across. Or to make themselves known. To scare us."

"*He* did this? Banks?" Emily's eyes were furious.

"It's okay. Stay calm." Liam lowered his head to look into her eyes. "He's already dead. And we're going to get rid of him. But I don't want you provoking him. He's capable of hurting you." His eyes traveled to her arm, indicating the scratches. "We're going to send him to the hell where he belongs. I promise."

Emily looked at Liam, fire still burning in them. "I'm sorry. I'm just so fucking tired of this."

"I know, baby. I think that's our cue to get this show started. Don't worry about the coffee. I'm ripping out that carpet anyway. Why don't you go to the van with Lexi? Make sure all of the cameras are visible on the monitors. You can brew some more coffee out there. Radio me when everything looks good, and we'll get started. I want you to calm down, and we'll bring you in later to help. Okay?"

Emily smoothed her hair back and inhaled. "Okay. I could use some fresh air."

Liam kissed her while Trey walked Lexi out to the van. Luke carried the spilled trays back to the kitchen.

"Besides the scratch, are you sure you're alright?" Liam asked while rubbing his hands up and down her arms. "That was quite a fall you took." On the surface, Liam fought to remain calm. But on the inside, his blood boiled. It was one thing to knock things over and show itself from afar. This time, it touched Emily, and Liam was seething. Banks was lucky he was already dead. The amount of anger stewing within him led him to believe he was capable of committing murder.

"I'm fine. Promise me we'll get rid of him. I want to move on from this."

"We will. I can't promise it will be tonight. I hope like fuck it will be. Otherwise, me and you are finding another place to live. But I promise I won't stop until he's gone." Liam kissed her again, only more passionately this time. Then he pulled away. "We're going to get started. We'll do some investigating first before we start digging. I'll bring you back in a little bit. There won't be any solo investigations this time. Things are just too unpredictable. It's best to stay together as a group."

"Okay. I'll be watching from the van. Be careful."

"Always." And Liam let her go. He watched as she reached the front door to the building where Trey held it open for her, and she proceeded down the steps to the van where Lexi was waiting for her.

"I forgot to ask you," Luke said. "Why do you want to investigate first? Shouldn't we start digging first?"

"I want to tear up that ground just as much as you do, brother. But I want to gather as much evidence as possible in case we do find a body or any bones and have to stop and call the police."

Luke nodded his head at his friend's explanation. "Where do we begin?"

Twenty-Seven

Emily tried to calm her nerves by watching Liam on the monitor. The night vision camera was trained on him as he walked around the basement with a camera in hand. She fiddled with her hands in her lap, trying to distract herself from the burning of the scratches left on her arm. She'd put Liam's jacket on, the one he always kept in the van, and with each breath she inhaled deeply to soak up his scent.

Thankful more than ever that Lexi was with her. She'd missed her. Lexi's companionship through their childhood had been Emily's one constant. The one element in her life that she could count on to stay the same.

"So. You and Liam seem pretty serious," Lexi stated while she poured a cup of coffee.

"Yeah," Emily said with a grin. "We are."

"Despite everything you told me that's happened since you've been here, you look so much more relaxed and so happy."

"I am happy. Liam is amazing. He's kind and thoughtful, and his parents and friends are incredible. With everything that's happened over the years, if I could go back and change anything, I wouldn't. I would keep it all the same because all of it led me to Liam."

Lexi smiled at her friend. "Em, did you sleep with him?"

Emily looked up. No verbal answer was needed. The smile and crimson color she felt taking hold of her face told her friend everything.

Lexi's eyes widened, and her eyebrows lifted. "Yeah?"

"Yes," Emily said, letting out a sigh of relief. She hadn't intentionally kept information from Lexi. The two just hadn't found time to connect long enough for her to confide in her friend. "I've never been more okay. It's weird. Even with all of this shit going on, I'm still happy. As long as I'm near Liam, everything is perfect. I don't know why, but it is. And I'm not letting this asshole of a ghost take that away from me."

"I'm so proud of you, Em. Promise me you'll stay positive. I know you'll get through this."

Emily nodded and took a sip of her coffee. When she looked up, she noticed Lexi fixated at the monitor that had Trey on camera. "So... You and Trey?"

Lexi shook her head and moved her attention away from the video screen. "I have no idea what you are talking about."

"Oh, come on!" Emily said. "I saw the look he gave you."

"What look? There was no look."

"I think he has the hots for you, girl."

"What!" Lexi said in disbelief. "He does not. We just met! He's nice, and I'll admit, good looking too. Really, good looking. But I don't have time for a relationship. Right now, my only focus is landing this job and finding a place to live. And, making sure you're okay."

Emily was about to respond, but Lexi held up her hand to stop her and pointed her attention to the gentleman walking toward them.

He was of average height, with dark skin, similar to Trey's complexion, and wore a jacket that featured a local sports team's logo.

"Good evening," he said as he reached the van. "I take it this is Liam's team's van. Liam sent me a text and told me you would be waiting here. I'm Dave Larson. They called and said they needed my help."

"Yes," Emily held out her hand to introduce herself. "I'm Emily, and this is my friend Lexi. Liam, Trey, and Luke are in the house. There was an incident a little while ago. They wanted us to wait in the van for a little bit while they got started. I can radio Liam and let them know you are here."

"Please do. Is everyone okay?"

Emily nodded. "Yes. Everyone is fine. A bit shaken up, but okay." She reached for the walkie talkie in the van and radioed Liam.

In a matter of seconds, Liam opened the front door to the building. "Dave!" he called out as he walked up to the man to hug him. "It's so good to see you."

"You too, Liam. Tell me. What is going on? This place feels so much heavier than the last time I was here."

***

Dave inhaled deeply as they passed the threshold of the house. "Liam, can I walk around first? There's a lot of energy here. I need to try and sort it out. Find out what exactly is going on."

"Of course. We are right behind you." Liam brought Dave up to speed with everything related to the haunting, but he purposely left out the information about who they believed the presence in the house was.

"Liam, this is not good. I don't know how I never picked up on it before. Emily, you moving in was definitely the catalyst of this presence waking up," Dave huffed out. He continued down the hall. "I don't need to go upstairs, Liam. Everything is centered down here, isn't it?"

"Yes," both Emily and Liam answered. Then Liam added, "The only time any activity happens upstairs is when Emily is up there with me."

Dave walked into Emily's flat. After circling around the living room, he stopped. "Okay. This is what I'm getting in here. It's definitely a male energy. He's not demonic. Although it might seem like it at times. He's powerful and possessive. His view on this is *'she's mine'*" Dave pointed at Emily, trying to convey what he was picking up. "He thinks you belong to him. He is adamant about that."

Liam asked, "Why now? Why haunt her to this extreme now after all of these years?"

Dave looked at his friend and said, "It's you. You are in the picture. You are her love, and he knows it. He's always known it. He's pacing back and forth, agitated. He's frustrated because as far as he's concerned, she's his, like a piece of property. And you stole her from him. We need to move downstairs. Is that possible?"

"Yes. Of course," Liam said as he led the way to the stairs to the basement.

Downstairs Trey and Luke were busy doing some EVP sessions. "Anything?" Liam asked.

"Nothing, man. It's totally quiet," Luke responded. "Dave, how are you?"

"Good, thanks. Guys, this spirit feels really unpredictable. He's possessive and can go into a rage at the flip of a switch. Be careful. He *is* here even though it seems quiet. He's right here, watching. I haven't felt a haunting this strong in a very long time."

Trey and Luke looked at Liam, surprised. Dave was already in full investigation mode, and he had only just arrived. Dave noticed the rented equipment to the side and immediately knew what the guys were planning on doing. "I have to tell you guys, you won't find any bodies here."

"You're certain?" Luke asked.

"I can feel it. They were here. You might find evidence of a grave, but you won't find bones."

"We are pretty sure we won't find anything either, but we want to be sure," Liam stated.

"I believe they were here at one time. Two of them. A man and a woman. But the earth was disturbed again and they were removed."

"Any idea where they might be now?"

"I don't know," Dave answered.

"I think we should dig anyway. Just to be one hundred percent sure." Trey suggested.

"I agree," Luke responded

"Me too." Emily looked at Liam. "We should dig. Even if it's only a little ways down. Just to make sure. I know what I've seen in my dreams. I just need to know."

"Okay," Liam told her.

"If it's okay with you guys," Dave spoke up, "I would like to stay for as long as possible. I feel like things will really pick up, and I don't want to leave you guys yet. I think he'll let me communicate with him at some point."

"Absolutely, Dave. Stay as long as you like. We really appreciate all of your help."

Luke, Trey, and Liam all grabbed shovels.

"Man, I am glad this floor is only dirt in here," Liam quipped as he began digging. "That son of a bitch has been enough of a pain in the ass lately. Having to bust through some concrete would have been even more of a pain in the ass."

They all laughed, including Emily and Dave.

"Don't provoke too much, Liam," Dave added.

"I'm not provoking, man. I'm just speaking the truth."

A while later, Liam and his teammates managed to move a few feet of dirt from the center of the room. The floor may have been dirt, but it was compacted and hard to work through. They stopped when something caught Luke's eye. He pointed to get everyone's attention. "Look there."

Liam bent down to move more loose dirt away from the area Luke pointed out. At first, he couldn't see what had caught his friend's eye until his hand touched what felt like damp, rough fabric. The realization that he was touching fabric caused his stomach to tighten into a knot. He wasn't sure if he wanted to continue at that point. Part of him wanted to grab Emily and run. Fuck the house renovations. Fuck the ghost. And fuck his plans. He just wanted to leave, didn't want his girl seeing whatever was lying beneath that dirt.

After taking a few breaths, he managed to calm his nerves. The thoughts that crossed his mind were an easy way out. Too easy. He knew the mother fucker would follow them. It had been tormenting Emily her entire life. There was no reason to think that it wouldn't continue to follow her. And now that he had found her, he was going to make sure Emily would be able to finally live her life in peace, and hopefully, he would be right by her side.

"Oh my god. Is that clothing?" Lexi whispered.

"Looks like it," Trey nodded and bent next to Liam. "Does it feel like it's attached or stuck to anything?"

"No. At least not yet." Liam resumed shoveling. Luke reached down and pulled the fabric once it seemed like it was uncovered enough to move. Liam was right. It wasn't attached to anything. It was a small, beige-colored lace sewn to another solid piece of fabric underneath. And it was clear that it had come from a piece of clothing.

Emily bent her knees and knelt on the dirt floor. Lexi was still standing next to her and bent with her, placing her hand on her shoulder. "Em, it's okay."

Liam was up and out of the ditch in seconds. "What's wrong, baby?"

"It's Abigail's," Emily spoke and with her trembling shoulders hunched over.

"She's right," Dave confirmed. That belonged to a woman. But she's not here anymore. Neither is the man. They were moved. But they died here. I know that for sure."

Liam looked at his friends and back to Dave. "I know. We know."

Luke walked to the corner of the room where they had placed some of their equipment while they were digging and picked up what looked like a small, round device that looked like a speaker.

"What is that?" Lexi asked with a shaky breath.

"It's what we call a spirit box," Luke answered. "It's similar to the voice recorder, only we can actually hear a spirit come through in real-time. So, there's no delay in reviewing the audio. We can ask questions and hopefully get a response immediately. It's going to be loud because it scans frequencies. So, we will hear a lot of white noise. And if we are lucky, this assholes voice will come through."

Luke switched on the device, and just like he had explained, the room was filled with the sound of static. He held the device out to Liam, and he took it from his friend. Liam asked, "Who are you?"

To everyone's shock, a voice immediately came through. A deep one who both Emily and Liam recognized. Emily paled. Liam hugged her tighter, trying to keep his anger under control when the voice replied, "James."

Liam felt sick. He had encountered many entities in his years of doing paranormal work—even demonic and dangerous ones. But none had ever given him the feeling of dread like this one. His skin broke out in a sweat, and his stomach churned, nauseating him. The anger he'd brought under control from earlier in the evening rose to the surface. The only thing that helped keep it in check was that he knew the end was near for this spirit. He had his best friends and Dave. He knew they had his back—both his and Emily's.

"Banks." Liam gathered all of his will power to tamp down his fear and anger once more. The last thing he wanted to have happen was for Emily to see him scared. But he was scared. Down to his core, he was terrified and pissed the fuck off too. He blew out a breath and managed to speak with a clear and calm voice. "Why are you still here?"

"You stole her from me." The voice came through, clear.

Liam answered, "No. She was never yours."

"She was mine," it growled.

"You lied to her. You killed Abigail's parents just to get to her." Now, Liam was yelling. His hands shook with the adrenaline pumping through his veins.

"She *is* mine."

"I was never yours," Emily shouted. Her voice shaky but stern. "You took my life and the life of the man I loved. You're a monster."

"Good girl." Liam leaned into her and whispered in her ear. "You heard her, Banks. Over a hundred years later, and she still feels the same. And so do I. We found each other again. You still lose. You will never have her."

"I'll have her."

"You're dead, Banks. You may be haunting this house, but you're still dead. We are alive, and you're going to leave us alone."

A frightening growl then came through the audio of the spirit box. Liam turned off the box. He looked at Emily and held her close. "Dave?"

"Right here."

"What do you suggest? How do we get rid of this son of a bitch?"

Dave bent his head and closed his eyes for a few moments before looking back up at his friend. "He feels conflicted. Mentally, when he was alive, he wasn't right in the head, for lack of a better term. He was always conflicted. Knowing what he wanted to do wasn't right, but he couldn't help it. He was mentally unstable and knows what he's been doing by haunting Emily isn't right. Knows what he did was wrong. But he doesn't know any other way to be. I think doing a cleansing will work. I know it doesn't seem like it, but he's scared and is worried about what he will encounter once he moves on. This place has become his safety zone. He was trapped in this house?"

"Yes," Liam confirmed. "Phil stated in his note that a seer trapped him here, to keep him contained. I have a feeling she was more of a witch. He mentioned spells and that she put one on Phil as a boy to keep him alive. Phil was the son of Charles, Banks' Butler."

"Oh. My. God," Dave said in disbelief. "Okay. This is making more sense to me now."

"What do you mean?" Trey asked.

"I've been seeing flashes of a woman. Not Abigail, another woman. I think she may be the seer Phil is referring to. She left these images specifically for me. She's showing me that her spell can be broken. That Banks can be released from this house if I can convince him to move on."

Everyone looked to one another as Dave spoke words containing a glimmer of hope. "Because he's so strong, Emily, he was able to keep an eye on you. He wants to continue controlling you even from afar. He still feels like he has the right to be possessive over you. It will take a lot of convincing, but I feel like I may be able to move him to the other side."

Twenty-Eight

"What's the plan?" Liam stated in a half growl when he entered his living room where everyone had gathered. He hadn't meant to sound brash, but he couldn't help it if he tried. His only concern at that moment was getting through the rest of the night and sending Banks to wherever the hell he needed to go was. He wanted to move on with his life with Emily. He'd left her in the bedroom of his flat with Lexi. The sight of the marks Banks had put on her killed him.

Luke looked up and put his finger to his lips in a hushed motion. That's when he noticed Dave sitting in the corner of the room, meditating. He'd seen Dave in this state before and knew he was preparing for what was to come. Dave needed to ground himself and gather energy. This was going to be a hell of a fight.

Liam sat in a chair next to Trey and Luke. The three men huddled close together and spoke in a whispered tone.

"Dave is going to open a portal and try to move Banks toward the light."

Liam nodded.

"This is going to be intense. Not just because Dave feels the need to prepare like he is, but we haven't come in contact with as powerful an entity as Banks in a long time. He's not going to go without a fight."

"I agree," Liam told his friend.

"Liam?" Luke spoke. "I know this is a personal case for you. For us. But I have to ask, do you want us to continue to roll the cameras and equipment and gather evidence. Because we'll understand if you want to keep this private?"

"Hell fucking yes," Liam replied. "I appreciate your guys' concern, but this is still a case. We gather evidence. All of it and treat it like we do all of our cases, with confidentiality and respect."

The sight of Dave making his way over to them caught their attention. "Liam, I think it goes without saying that this is going to be hard. Banks is agitated. He may lash out. He has the power to physically harm the living. I need to warn all of you that it is more than likely he will become violent during this. And as much as I hate to insist that Emily be present, I think it's necessary."

Liam's instinct was to tell Dave absolutely not. But knowing Emily and not wanting to take her power and decisions from her, he knew it would have to be entirely her decision. "I'll talk to her."

"Good." Dave rubbed his hands together, vigorously. "We should get started soon."

"Why don't you guys head back downstairs? Do one more check of all the cameras. I don't want to miss anything. Make sure we have extra charged batteries ready to go in case anything is drained while we are down there."

"Got it." Trey stood. "I'll wait for Lexi. I'll get her settled back out in the van. I don't think it's a good idea for her to be near the investigation at this point. She'll be safer in the van."

Liam agreed and got up from the chair. He made his way down the narrow hallway and could barely hear the women talking in the bedroom, their voices muffled by the closed door. He knocked softly, and their voices ceased, followed by a voice he recognized as Emily's telling him to come in. Lexi had already made her way to the door and smiled as she passed Liam.

"Trey is waiting for you. He'll fill you in on the plan."

"Okay." She continued down the hallway.

Liam closed the door behind him, and in three steps, made his way to the bed where Emily sat. The covers draped over her legs. She looked a little rested. A warm smile graced her face.

Knowing they had work to do, he couldn't help the overwhelming need to kiss her. When he reached the bed, he climbed over her and crashed his mouth onto hers. Devouring every inch of her. Liam knew he took her by surprise, but she quickly relaxed and kissed him back with just as much enthusiasm.

Liam wanted so much more, and as much as he hated the blanket between them, he was glad there was a barrier. Had there not been, he was sure he would have taken Emily right then, and they needed to get downstairs with the rest of the team.

Liam slowed their kiss when she whimpered. His body lay cradled between her legs on top of the blanket still, and he gave her a small thrust of his hips. He moved his mouth from hers, both of them gasping for air, and left a trail of kisses down her jaw to her neck. He made his way up to her ear and nipped the tip with his teeth.

"Baby," he rasped before lifting his head and looking at her. "I promise, later, I will make love to you all night. But not right now. Dave is going to attempt to move Banks toward the light. He thinks he can help him move on. He wants you to be there. Thinks you can be of help. Telling Banks again that you're not his.

"But baby, I have to warn you. He also said he might get violent. He's already pissed, and with Dave opening up the door for him to move on will probably piss him off even more. It will get intense. I wanted to tell Dave no, you weren't going anywhere near that room. But I know this has to be your decision. I'll be right by your side the whole time. I just want you to know this will get ugly."

"Are you scared?" Emily asked.

"Me? Fuck yes. We don't always call Dave in for help. Only in the most extreme circumstances. I trust him. So, if he tells me things could get dangerous, I take that to heart. Except this time, it involves you. And that's killing me."

"I love you, Liam." Emily blurted out.

The warmth of her words washed over him, his heart exploded. "I love you too, Em. I've loved you always. In this life and in my last."

Emily reached up and brought Liam's head down to meet hers. She kissed him again, only this time more passionately. There wasn't any desperation this time. This time it was truly a kiss of two lovers.

A soft knock echoed through the bedroom. Breaking their kiss, Liam turned his head slightly to respond. "Yep?"

"We're ready when you guys are," Luke's voice came through the door.

"We'll be right there."

A thought crossed Liam's mind then. "What's your decision, babe?"

"Huh?" Emily asked, confused. Liam saw she was still lost in the passionate kiss they had just shared.

"You never told me if you want to be there with us or if you want to stay in the van. Instead, you declared your love for me. Which I am so fucking happy about. But I still need to know. What's your decision?"

Twenty-Nine

"Cameras are rolling. Audio is rolling. Everything seems to be working great," Trey told Liam and Emily as they entered the basement. He lifted a walkie talkie to his mouth and spoke. "Lexi, do you copy?"

"Yes, I copy."

Emily caught the grin on Trey's face when her voice came through. "We're getting started."

"Copy that."

Emily stood in the middle of the room. "It feels heavy," she spoke softly. "Does that make any sense?"

"It sure does," Luke confirmed.

"He knows what we are planning." Dave lifted his head and made eye contact with everyone. "We should get started." Dave stood in the middle of the room next to Emily and Liam. "I'm going to speak to him. You two feel free to speak up at any time."

Emily grabbed hold of Liam's hand. Her heart pounded with anticipation. Her eyes adjusted slowly to the low light in the room. Her ears strained to hear any unfamiliar sound, and her skin crawled at any slight breeze, the sensation heightened by her hairs standing on end.

"Robert Banks," Dave began. "I know you're here. It's time you listen and understand that your time on this Earth is done. It's been done for a very long time. You need to move on."

Dave stood with his eyes closed, his head tipped up toward the ceiling. The air in the room bared down on the group with an electrical charge. As if a lightning storm was imminent.

"Trey?" Liam said. "Get the spirit box ready. I have a feeling we're going to need it."

Trey grabbed the spirit box from the corner of the room and turned it on. The room was engulfed in the sounds of static, but no voices were audible. Liam decided to speak. "Banks," he said with irritation in his voice. "It's time you leave. You're dead. You can't have Emily. She's alive. You've been dead for a very long time. You need to move on."

Coldness crept up from the ground at Liam and Emily's feet. The air, like ice moving upward, washed over them. A cold so bitter it took Emily's breath from her. She watched Liam go pale. "Are you okay?" she whispered.

"It just got really cold."

Emily was still holding Liam's hand when a force grabbed her, yanking her out of Liam's grasp, and pulled her to the side towards the far corner of the room. An explosion erupted, the entire room shook, and they were engulfed in a blinding light. She skidded across the dirt floor at an unnatural speed and came to a stop at the cinderblock wall at the far corner. The air had been knocked out of her, and she tried desperately to catch her breath.

When she opened her eyes, she glimpsed at Liam across the room. He had been thrown to the opposite wall, and Dave could barely keep his footing but somehow managed to crouch down and stay upright. Trey and Luke huddle together in the door, still holding their equipment. A deafening whirlwind of bitter cold swirled around.

"Liam!" Luke shouted. "Something is holding us back. We can't get past the door."

"I can't move!" Liam told them. "Emily! Are you okay?"

Emily tried desperately to speak, but her voice was caught in her throat. Above her stood the transparent silhouette of Robert Banks. A form she had never seen him take in this life. She had only seen his features in her nightmare. He wore the same long, black coat and carried the same heavy walking stick as he did in all of her dreams. He looked down at her with a scowl. Emily felt nothing but hate emanating from him. Banks knelt next to her, and she felt the icy touch of his hand on her cheek. She shivered uncontrollably. From the bitter cold or fear, she couldn't be sure. Her body went numb from the chill. In her head, she was screaming for him to leave, but no matter how hard she tried, she couldn't make her lips move.

Luke made his way into the room but just barely. The sound of the spirit box still pulsing but muffled by the windstorm around them. Emily caught movement in the corner of her eye. Dave managed to crawl toward her. He stared at the transparent form above her.

"Banks!" Dave yelled. "Step away from her. You can't have her."

"Get away from her!" Liam desperately pleaded.

"Please," she managed to finally speak. "Leave me. I don't want to be with you. You can't have me. You have to move on."

Those few words were all Emily could manage. She was exhausted, her body weighed down with the oppression hovering over her. The smell of damp dirt flooded her nose. Images from when Banks' men threw her in a shallow grave crept into her mind. She knew what was happening. The life was being pulled from her. She knew because she had felt it before, and at that moment, she decided she was not dying at the hands of Banks again. Emily prayed she could find the strength to fight and tried to speak again.

"I'm not going with you!" she yelled, mustering all the power she could to enunciate her words. "Go to hell where you belong!"

The icy touch she felt on her cheek earlier was now around her neck. Emily tried to get up, but she was paralyzed. She could faintly hear Liam and Dave yelling in the background, but she couldn't focus on their words. All she could concentrate on was her vision going dark.

Thirty

The son of a bitch was choking Emily, and Liam couldn't do a fucking thing about it. He had never been a violent person, but at that moment, he wanted nothing more than to kill Banks with his bare hands. Too bad the bastard was already dead.

He was screaming but couldn't make his body move. A force held him in one spot while he watched in agony as Banks hovered over Emily with his hands around her neck. The realization that he may not get to her in time was closing in on him. "Dave! What can we do? He's going to kill her!"

Dave was on his knees in the middle of the room with his eyes closed. Liam knew he was trying to communicate with Banks. He also knew that it wasn't working. Liam prayed. Tears streaming from his eyes, he prayed to god—all of the gods—anyone above who was listening to help him. He closed his eyes and heard his father's words.

"What you allow is what will continue."

"Dad?" He'd heard his father speak those words to him his entire life. Only now he knew that voice wasn't his father's. It was familiar, but he couldn't put his finger on who it was.

"Fight!"

"There's a voice trying to come through the spirit box. I can't make out what it's trying to say," Trey shouted.

"It's family. It's his family," Dave yelled.

As soon as Liam heard Dave's words, a glimmer of hope washed over him, and he spoke to his old friend. "Phil. It's Phil," he told the rest of his team. Liam concentrated, gathered all of his strength, and brought himself onto his hands and knees. He made his way to Dave, who gestured that he was okay, then he crawled his way across the room. Through the raging windstorm that encircled Emily. He pulled her onto his lap. Her eyes were closed as he pressed two fingers to the side of her neck. There was a faint pulse under the tips of his fingers. He looked to his friends in the doorway, who he gave a nod to. Both Luke and Trey nodded back in a silent exchange of his confirmation that Emily was alive.

"Banks, please. Let her go. Go with Phil to the light. He's here to help you. He's your kin, your family. He'll take care of you. You have to let Emily go. Please." Liam hoped to all that was holy that his plea to Banks would work.

"It's working," Dave shouted. "He's backing away."

Liam looked at Emily as she took a deep breath. Her eyes were still closed, but she was alive and breathing.

"Come, cousin. It's time to come with me," Liam heard Phil's voice through the spirit box.

"What will happen to me?" A gruff voice, different from Phil's, came through, and Liam knew it was Banks.

"I don't know. But you can't stay here. This isn't the answer," Phil replied. "Now. Come with me. Let them be."

"He's moving on. He's going toward the light." Dave looked up and gave a small smile to Liam.

"Phil," Liam shouted with desperation.

"Yes, Liam?"

Liam wasn't sure he would be able to speak. He was being flooded with so many emotions he wasn't sure he could find the words. He breathed deeply, swallowing past the lump in his throat, and said, "Thank you. For everything."

"Take care, Liam. All of you," Phil's voice came through again but was faint and had carried more static. But the team had used the spirit box enough over the years that they could decipher the voice's message.

"Thanks, Phil."

Luke and Trey stated in unison. The air around the team settled. At last, they could hear each other. The room had gone quiet.

"Is everyone okay?" Liam asked.

He received a nod from Dave.

Luke and Trey rushed to their feet and ran to him. "How's Emily?" Trey asked.

Liam stared down at her and stroked her face. Her red-rimmed lids fluttered open. "Hey," he said.

"Hey," she croaked, then cleared her throat.

"Tell me the truth. Are you okay? Does anything hurt?" Liam asked her, firmly.

"I think I'm okay. I'm sore, but nothing feels broken. But my head is pounding."

"I saw you hit your head when you were thrown back to the wall," Luke stated.

"Alright. Let's go." Liam stood up, scooping Emily into his arms, and walked out of the small room.

"Liam, I can walk."

"Nope." He could tell that his short answer irritated her. In the back of his mind, he kicked himself for acting like a caveman, but he couldn't help it. He'd lost the love of his life once. He wasn't about to lose her again. He was taking Emily to the hospital to be checked out whether she liked it or not. And he was prepared to fight her on the matter if it came down to it.

At the top of the stairs, in the hallway on the main level, Liam sat on one of the steps leading up to his apartment. "Look at me, babe."

Emily turned her gaze to him.

"I want to get you checked out at the hospital. Luke said you hit your head, and you told me you have a bad headache. I want to make sure you don't have a concussion. So, we will go get you checked out, just to make sure. Okay?"

"I'm really okay," she argued.

"Baby, listen. I'm not losing you again. Will you do me a favor? Humor me, yeah? Go to the hospital. Let me hear the doctor say you're okay, and I'll bring you back here. Please."

Dave brought up the rear of the group, and when he passed by Liam, he stopped to check on Emily.

"She says she's okay, but we're going to the hospital to get her checked out. Her head is still hurting, and I want to make sure she doesn't have a concussion."

"Smart," Dave told Liam as he knelt down, putting himself at eye level with both Liam and Emily. He stared intensely at them. "He's gone. I felt him cross over. And your friend, Phil, he went with him. You're free now. Both of you."

"He went to the light?" Emily asked.

"Yes, he'll face his judgment. I'm a true believer in that."

Emily threw her arms around Dave and hugged him. Liam threw his free arm around Dave as well and whispered, "Thank you."

Dave nodded. "If you two ever need anything, you call me. No matter what the time."

"We will," both Liam and Emily stated, and Dave stood to head toward the front door. Liam watched as Lexi bolted between Trey and Luke and beelined for her best friend.

"Em! Are you okay? The cameras went out after that burst of light. What was that? Why are you sitting down? What's wrong?"

"Easy, Lex," Liam soothed. "She hit her head when she was thrown to the back wall. We were all thrown across the room when you saw that flash of light. I'm taking her to the hospital to get checked out. I'm sure she's fine, but I want to make sure."

"I'm going with you."

"No," Emily interrupted. "You've had a long day. I want you to get settled. You can stay in my flat because I'll be staying upstairs with Liam. Stay here, get settled, and rest, so we can hang out and talk tomorrow. Liam is with me, and he'll keep you updated." Emily looked at Liam for confirmation that he would update Lexi. He gave both women a smile and a nod.

"Okay. But if anything happens, you call me!" Lexi held out her hand and pointed at him.

"I will, Lex. I'll take good care of her." Liam stood, still holding Emily in his arms. He proceeded to walk to the front door.

Thirty-One

A month had passed since the night of the investigation. And since that night, there had been no sign of Banks. Emily no longer felt the ominous presence that she had grown accustomed to her entire life. She hadn't even known what it felt like to truly be relaxed. She no longer had the faint feeling of someone watching over her every move.

Emily had moved into Liam's flat for good that night. After the doctors at the hospital had diagnosed her with a minor concussion, they discharged her and told her to come back if her headaches didn't improve. Liam spent the rest of that night and most of the next day letting her sleep, only waking her up periodically to make sure she knew her name, who he was, and what year it was. Then he would let her fall asleep again.

Liam's parents had come to see them both a few days after. Janet had brought enough prepared meals with her to last both of them a month. She put them in the freezer and told them she would be back in a couple of weeks to restock their refrigerator. Janet had called a couple weeks after and asked if they needed anything. Liam had been out of town on an investigation, so Emily decided to head down to Carmel to visit on her own. She spent the entire day talking mostly with Janet. She was comfortable being around Liam's parents. They were sweet and funny, and everything she imagined good parents would be.

Liam's apartment was beginning to feel like home. Home. That was something she had never felt before. And the thought made her eyes flood with tears every time she thought about it. Liam gave her permission to decorate however she wanted. "Make this place feel like the home you've always wanted," and now that was exactly what she was doing.

She decided to keep the oversized sofa. It was incredibly comfortable, and the color was a perfect neutral dark grey, so she could add touches of color in other areas of the room. Plus, it had some great memories attached to it now. She smiled and felt her cheeks flush at the thought of them on the sofa, kissing until breathless and the memory of the first time Liam made love to her there. Yeah, they were definitely keeping that sofa.

Liam had been surprised and relieved when Emily told him she wanted to keep it. He confessed that he really didn't want to move the enormous sectional back down the narrow stairs and was sure his friends would wring his neck if he asked them to help move it again. Liam had burst into a fit of laughter when the memory crossed his mind, and he had to explain to Emily that it had truly been like the scene from *Friends* when Ross buys a couch and he and Chandler are trying to move it up a flight of stairs.

Emily was sitting on the large sofa, lounging against one of the arms, propped up with pillows when Liam walked in. She hadn't heard him come through the door, which was a testament to how comfortable she had become. Before Liam, she was used to constantly scanning her surroundings and picking up the slightest noises. But now, she was carefree. Enjoying life, the way she always should have been able to enjoy it.

***

Liam stopped and stared at Emily. Her legs were bent, supporting her laptop while she worked with earbuds in. Her head swayed gently to the music she was listening to. A hint of a smile crossed her lips. He'd just gotten back from a long day of meetings and running errands. One of those errands involved a trip to an antique shop with his two best friends, and the sizable purchase was nestled in its protective case inside the small bag he held. He'd also stopped at the store for a bottle of wine and a bouquet of flowers.

Liam set everything on the kitchen counter and made his way through the living room. Emily still hadn't noticed him since she was engrossed in her work. When he stepped into her view, she looked up with a huge smile. "When did you get home?" she asked as she pulled her earbuds out.

"Just now," Liam leaned down and placed a kiss on her lips. Then he positioned himself behind her, so her back was to his front, and nuzzled her neck. "Something smells good."

"I made Eggplant Parmesan."

"Seriously?" His mouth watered as the delicious smell filled the flat.

"Yes," Emily said in a half giggle. "I asked your mom for her recipe. It was surprisingly easy to prepare. How was your day?"

"Fucking awesome. I'll tell you all about it at dinner."

Liam stood and held his hand out to help Emily off the couch. He opened the bottle of wine in the kitchen while Emily plated up the Eggplant Parmesan and garlic bread. While they ate, Liam told her about the plans that he and Luke's cousin, a building engineer, had come up with.

"Really? We can do all of that?" she asked.

"It's expensive, but it can be done. We'll move the stairwell and reinforce everything. Then, we can push this hole wall back and widen the living room. That will give us space for one extra bedroom here in the front. And with everything being pushed out, we can also split the back bedroom into two. This will be a three-bedroom flat."

"That sounds amazing."

"Yes, it does. Are you excited?"

"Yes! I can't wait. Lexi says she'll be moving up to Napa next week. So, we can stay downstairs if we need to while work is being done up here."

"That works out perfectly." Liam took her hand in his as he sipped his wine. "I wanted to get the upstairs done first before we start downstairs. How is Lex? Is she excited?"

"Yes, she is. She gets to work at a wine resort and live on property. It's her dream come true. What's in the bag?" Emily asked, noticing the bag on the counter.

Liam grinned at her. "It's a surprise."

Emily's eyes lit up with excitement. Liam stood, grabbing her by the hand, and pulled her to him. He kissed the hell out of her right there in the kitchen, leaving Emily squirming. When he pulled away and looked down at her, she was breathless. "What was that?"

"That was a kiss. Let's go to bed." Liam pulled her toward the hallway. He made sure he grabbed the bag and carried it into the bedroom.

Giggling, Emily said, "It's only 7:30 at night."

"Good. More time for me to explore your body."

Heat flashed in Emily's eyes, and Liam continued guiding her to their bedroom, where Liam ripped his shirt off and hauled Emily's over her head. She worked on the buckle on his jeans, and Liam had her yoga pants down over her hips in point two seconds before they both hit the bed. He took his time stripping off Emily's bra and panties, kissing his way down her body until his head settled between her legs. Every time she was close, he pulled away and slowed his actions. Keeping her on the brink for what felt like hours. "Liam! You're killing me."

He smiled against her. At Emily's soft whimper, he gave her what she needed and relished in her moans of pleasure. A sound he couldn't seem to get enough of. In seconds, Liam removed the rest of his clothes before climbing over her again, settling on top of her. Emily arched her back, and Liam grabbed her hand. Her eyes were closed as he slipped the ring onto the tip of her finger.

When she looked at her hand resting in his, she caught the glimmer of the gold ring as he finished pushing it up past her knuckle. Her eyes locked with his, a flood of tears already streaming out of them. "Tell me those are happy tears, baby."

"Liam? How did you?" she breathed out. Her lower lip quivered as she stared at him.

"You know that antique shop around the corner?" Emily nodded as she sucked in a breath. "I was walking past it a few days ago and walked in to have a look around. It was sitting there, in the glass case, right in front. I put money down on it then so the owner would hold it for me. I went back this afternoon and paid the balance."

Liam had instantly recognized the ring. It was the same one he had slipped on Abigail's finger moments before Banks barged in and removed it from her. The gold band still shining with its engraved details. The center cut amethyst stone was surrounded by six smaller diamonds that sparkled brilliantly. "The shop owner said it's been in the store for years. No one has ever been interested in it."

Emily squeezed her eyes shut as more tears escaped from beneath her eyelids. "It's beautiful. It's just how I remember it."

"Baby, the first time I saw you, those eyes, those beautiful brown eyes captivated me. My whole life, I've been searching not only for evidence of life after death but for a meaning to the life I'm living right now. In my line of work, I see fear, anxiety and deal with the subject of death every day. Sometimes Evil. I spent my days in a semi-state of fogginess, just going through the motions of life—a never-ending loop of too many questions but not enough answers. I spent my days desperately searching for the truth to all the unanswered questions, not knowing if I'll ever be able to find them.

"Then you walked into this building, and everything clicked. You're the answer to some of those questions. When I look at you, all I see is beauty. You remind me of all the beauty and good there is in the world. You remind me that no matter how fucked up life can be, there is always a brighter side. There's always a chance to start over. To start again. We shouldn't spend our life only questioning our existence on this Earth. We should also enjoy this life and all its little moments. You're my Windflower that I captured. You floated in here on a soft, heavenly breeze. You stood up to a ghost who lived a life filled with evil deeds and did unthinkable things. You gave me the courage to stand up and fight him too.

"You're it for me, and I'm not letting go. In my past life, in this life, and I'm gonna search for you in my next life too."

"Never in a million years did I ever think words that sweet and heartfelt would be spoken to me—about me," Emily whispered as tears streamed down her face. "You're it for me too, Liam. I'm yours, and you're mine. There's no doubt in my mind or my heart about that."

"Marry me, baby. Spend the rest of your life with me. I promise I'll spend the rest of my life cherishing you and relishing in all the beauty and fighting all the demons that this life throws at us."

Emily nodded. Liam kissed her damp cheeks. "Yes," she finally managed to whisper.

"Yes?"

"Yes," she repeated. "Yes, I'll marry you, Liam."

"Soon?" Liam asked while pushing inside of her. Emily arched her back and wrapped her legs around his waist, locking her ankles at his back.

"Soon," she assured. "Now, please, make love to me."

"Always," Liam whispered.

Thirty-Two

"Man, you should have seen your face! It was epic."

"Dude, shut up!" Liam shouted playfully.

"Serious, Emily. Lexi, it's hilarious now, but we were seriously scared shitless. Literally," Luke told the group, still in a fit of laughter.

"I was not," Trey iterated.

"Well, I was!" Luke admitted.

Everyone at the table was in tears of laughter. They had laughed all through dinner while listening to some of the stories of encounters the guys had come into contact with over the years. Mostly stories from their days when they first began investigating and how unprepared they were for what they came in contact with.

"Seriously, guys. I shit my pants that night. Liam, did you shit your pants?"

Liam could only nod his head as he tried to catch his breath. "I did a little. Yeah," he managed.

"I knew it. See, Trey. Liam admitted it. He shit his pants too. You still gonna sit there and say you didn't shit your pants after a goddamn shadow figure peaked its head around the corner then slammed that prison cell door on our second investigation?"

"Come on, Trey, you can tell us the truth. We won't judge," Lexi said while taking a sip of her drink.

"I did not shit my pants." Grumbles followed before he went on to say, "However! However, I did piss myself a little."

"I knew it!" Luke said while slamming his hand down on the table.

"You pissed yourself a lot, didn't you?" Liam asked.

"Yep," Trey admitted, still laughing and nodding his head. "Yeah, I pissed my pants."

After a couple of minutes, when everyone had composed themselves, Liam put his arm around Emily and pulled her close to him. "Listen, other than the fact that Emily and I love you guys and your all family to us and we missed you and wanted to share a meal with you, we asked you guys to meet us here because we have something we want to tell you."

Silence ensued amongst everyone. Liam took in the look on his friends' faces, then turned and said, "I asked Emily to marry me."

"*Oh my god!*" Lexi shouted, slamming both palms to her face.

After a beat, Emily ended the suspense. "I said…*yes!*"

An eruption of cheers and congratulations followed. Everyone hugged each other. There were tears of happiness and squealing from both women. Even the other patrons dining around them cheered along with them as they heard the good news. Their waitress had even brought over another round of drinks for them. "On the house, you guys. Congratulations!" She smiled at everyone as she set the drinks down.

"When's the big day?" Was the next round of questions.

"We don't know yet. We don't want to wait too long." Emily wiped happy tears from her eyes.

"Yeah," Liam continued, "I think we've waited long enough. As soon as we find a venue, we're booking the first date they have available."

"How about the winery?"

Emily turned to her friend. "The winery does weddings?"

"Yes. Of course, they do. And guess who is in charge of all the bookings? And the vendors?" Lexi said in a sing-song voice.

Emily threw her hands to her face in excitement. "Are you serious?"

"Yes! Tell me a date, and if there aren't any other events that day, I'll put it on the books for you and get the contract drawn up."

Emily looked at Liam, she smiled ear to ear. "We haven't seen that particular winery yet." The two of them had made their way around wine country, stopping and staying a night at different resorts, but had mostly stuck to the larger wineries. They hadn't yet ventured into the hills where they knew some hidden gems were secretly nestled away.

"I'm sure it will be perfect. I trust Lexi's judgment. If she thinks it will be a perfect place for our wedding and you want to do it. Then let's book it."

"You guys," Lexi cut in, "it's beautiful. It's in the hills and surrounded by trees. The grapevines are a few miles down the road at another location. The actual resort is so romantic. There's a brook that runs around the property. It will make for the most beautiful photos. We have a list of preferred vendors I can give you, so you don't have to shop around for florists or caterers unless you want to. But I've been reading up on the vendors we work with and have met a few of them, and they are really great. Plus, there are a ton of suites on the property, so you guys can stay the night of the wedding before you head off on your honeymoon."

"October?" Emily asked abruptly.

"October is perfect," Lexi said. "And oh my god. Emily, the trees will be changing colors. It's perfect!"

"October it is," Liam agreed.

"We're getting married!" Emily squealed.

Liam looked around the table where they all sat in the corner of the restaurant. In a few short months, Emily had gone from being essentially alone to moving to a new city, facing demons, and learning about who she was in a past life. He admired her courage and strength and couldn't be more proud of her. And he made sure he told her that every day.

Liam still had days where he couldn't believe he had found the woman who had haunted his dreams for years. And he fell in love with her. Again. Now, instead of the two of them dreaming about the other, they were together. And there was going to be a wedding. He was going to marry his true love. The thought made his chest burst even more. Every time he looked at Emily, she took his breath away. And now, she was going to be his wife.

His team's business was busier than ever. He made a mental note to block off time at the end of August and most of September so he could be around more to help with the wedding planning if needed. Lexi was a godsend, and he pretty much considered her his sister-in-law now.

They would also be remodeling their new headquarters and home. They had talked about moving to an actual house outside of the city and had decided that they would get through the remodeling first before they started looking. That way, the flat would be all ready for a renter whenever they wanted to move.

He hadn't told Emily yet, but he really couldn't wait to start filling that flat with babies. They had talked about a family and agreed that after the wedding they would start trying. But he had to admit, he would be ecstatic if Emily happened to end up pregnant sooner rather than later.

Liam's parents were overjoyed when they called to tell them the news of their engagement. Liam's mom cried and couldn't stop telling them how happy she was. She was also already in constant contact with

Emily every day. The two of them sent pictures from Pinterest back and forth to each other, all related to wedding planning.

His dad was ecstatic about having another daughter join the family. He even commented that the beach house in Carmel might be getting too small for the growing family. With most of his siblings married and new grandchildren being born, his dad mentioned he may need to invest in a wine country resort to accommodate everyone.

Liam laughed at his dad's comment, but deep down, he knew Clayton Wesley was probably already looking into new properties. Most likely, old wine resorts or a vineyard in the hills that he could take over.

Liam would miss going down to the beach, but he had to admit, he loved wine country just as much.

Epilogue

Trey Donovan drove home after dinner with his friends that night. His mind continually drifted back to the way Lexi looked. God, she was gorgeous. She was shorter than Emily by a few inches, but her personality overshot her height by a few feet. She was edgy, with her dark pixie cut and bold makeup that set her eyes ablaze. She was confident and witty. But he could sense she had a bit of a delicate side there too. A side that she tried desperately to hide.

He'd seen her quite a few times over the past month since she stayed in Emily's old flat, and the team got together quite often to talk business. And since she and Emily were pretty much inseparable, he managed to run into Lexi a few times a week. And every time he saw her, she burrowed her way into him a little more.

The reminder that she was moving up to Napa to the resort that she took a job at shot through him and his heart ached at the idea. He was sure he'd run into her plenty since she was best friends with Emily, but he was going to miss not seeing her as much as he already was. He had toyed with the idea lately about asking her on a date, but something told him to hold off.

One evening while at Liam and Emily's, he overheard Lexi telling her friend how she just couldn't bring herself to date anyone because she didn't want to get hurt. It was easier to just "stay single and not worry about the possible heartache that comes with dating." Those were her words. His heart just about stopped when he heard her utter them. So, he held off simply because he was trying to figure out a way to ask her without scaring her away.

What had Lexi gone through that would cause such a strong woman to basically swear off dating? Or, better yet, who in their right mind would hurt her so badly to cause her to feel apprehension about being with anyone. It was a question that he was determined to get to the bottom of. To figure out the source of her fear and hopefully change her mind.

Next up is Trey and Lexi's story, coming in 2021

Acknowledgement

To my husband, thank you for supporting me on this journey. For taking the kids out so I could have some quiet time to write. For letting me vent and break down as I figured out how to navigate this life of becoming an indie author. I love you.

To Piper Kennedy, you're the best!

To all of my followers and supporters, thank you for believing in me. This book would not have been possible without the excitement and enthusiasm you expressed. It's because of you that this book came to life. Thank you.

About the Author

Temperance Dawn discovered her love for writing in high school and has written on and off over the last couple of decades. She has written short stories over the years as well as a food blog. Her favorite genre for writing is Adult Romance in the sub-genre of Paranormal. Temperance fell in love with the Paranormal world at a young age and enjoys writing stories of strong characters overcoming adversity and fear, encountering the spiritual unknown, hauntings, ghostly apparitions, and tales of Vampires.

While her character's encounters with the spirit world are suspenseful and intriguing, there's always a romantic element to her stories. She's a believer in true love, and that everyone deserves a Happily Ever After.

Temperance is a wife and homeschooling mom to two rambunctious, beautiful kids. In her free time, she enjoys cooking, gardening, and taking long leisurely walks.

Let's stay in touch! I would love to hear from you.

My website is www.temperancedawn.com

Follow me on Instagram and Facebook @Authortemperancedawn